YORK NOTES

General Editors: Professor A.N. Jeffares (*University of Stirling*) & Professor Suheil Bushrui (*American University of Beirut*)

D.H. Lawrence

SONS AND LOVERS

Notes by Lance St John Butler

MA (CAMBRIDGE) PHD (STIRLING)
Lecturer in English Studies, University of Stirling

D1078652

LONGMAN
YORK PRESS

YORK PRESS
Immeuble Esseily, Place Riad Solh, Beirut.

ADDISON WESLEY LONGMAN LIMITED
Edinburgh Gate, Harlow,
Essex CM20 2JE, England
Associated companies, branches and representatives
throughout the world

First published 1980
Fifteenth impression 1997

ISBN 0-582-02308-4

Produced by Longman Singapore Publishers Pte Ltd
Printed in Singapore

Contents

Part 1: Introduction   *page* 5

  D.H. Lawrence   5

  Lawrence's literary and cultural background   8

  Lawrence as a poet   10

  The writing of *Sons and Lovers*   10

  A note on the text   11

Part 2: Summaries   12

  A general summary   12

  Detailed summaries: Part one   14

  Part two   26

Part 3: Commentary   45

  The author's own view of the book   45

  Sons and Lovers as autobiography   46

  The structure of *Sons and Lovers*   49

  The style of *Sons and Lovers*   51

  The characters in *Sons and Lovers*   57

  The main themes of *Sons and Lovers*   60

Part 4: Hints for study   64

Part 5: Suggestions for further reading   70

The author of these notes   71

Part 1

Introduction

D.H. Lawrence

The life of any great novelist is interesting but the life of D.H. Lawrence, for a student of *Sons and Lovers*, is almost an essential study. *Sons and Lovers* is a fictional version of Lawrence's own childhood and adolescence; the fiction follows the reality so closely that the novel almost seems to be an autobiography.

Like Paul Morel, David Herbert Lawrence was a younger child in a mining family living in a large village near Nottingham. He was born in 1885 in Eastwood (the 'Bestwood' of the novel). His mother, Lydia, was a proud and relatively refined and educated woman who came from a background somewhat superior to the mining community into which she married. She was not happy in her marriage and, once the energy and vitality of her husband had ceased to attract her, she seems to have found life with him very limited and unsatisfying.

Lawrence's father was perhaps not quite as rough as Morel in *Sons and Lovers*. Later in his life Lawrence saw that he had perhaps misjudged his father in the novel; after all, one of Lawrence's main beliefs was that the living and warm is better than the dead and cold, and his father was a vital and attractive character who seems to have been a good dancer as well as a great drinker of beer. However, there is no doubt that Lydia Lawrence was disappointed in her miner husband and that they had noisy arguments which frightened their children.

Lawrence's mother exerted a great influence on him. She encouraged his intellectual and artistic pursuits and helped him to go into the High School in Nottingham where he stayed until he was sixteen. In that year he met a girl called Jessie Chambers who is clearly the original of Miriam. Jessie lived with her parents and brothers on a farm, read romantic literature, attended chapel and had an idealised intellectual affair with young Lawrence which probably did not involve the physical love-making that occurs between Paul and Miriam in the novel.

After school Lawrence worked for a while in Haywood's surgical goods factory, on which Jordan's is based, and then decided to become a schoolmaster. He spent the four years 1902 to 1906 as a trainee teacher and then the two years 1906 to 1908 at Nottingham University College where he finally qualified as a teacher. His early interests were kept up during this training and he studied drawing and music (in which his mother had encouraged him), botany (Mrs Morel's pride in her garden and Paul's interest in flowers are marked in *Sons and Lovers*) and French (we are reminded of the French literature which Paul and Miriam study together).

In 1908 Lawrence accepted a job in a school in London and therefore, at the age of twenty-three, he left his home for almost the first time. This long period of close attachment to his mother, to his home and to the Eastwood mining community was crucial in Lawrence's development. He went on to write novels about all sorts of people and places, including Australia (*Kangaroo*) and Mexico (*The Plumed Serpent*), but his most successful and convincing work is undoubtedly that which has its roots in his English Midlands background. Perhaps of all his great English novels, including *Women in Love*, *The Rainbow* and *Lady Chatterley's Lover*, the greatest is *Sons and Lovers* because it is the closest to its author's own experience.

Sons and Lovers ends at the point where young Paul decides to go away from home; the end of the novel implies that at last his adolescence is coming to a close. In telling the story of Lawrence's life after his move to London, therefore, I am beginning to go beyond the limits of our novel.

Lawrence's first publication was in 1909 when the *English Review* printed some of his poems. Then in 1911 his first novel, *The White Peacock*, appeared. It was something of a success although neither of Lawrence's parents appreciated this: his mother was dying of cancer, in circumstances very similar to those of Mrs Morel, and only lived long enough to have a copy of the novel placed in her hands. His father was shocked by the amount of money the publishers had paid for the book (£50) and complained that his son had hardly worked hard enough to deserve this much. But while his novel, together with his poems and some short stories, were earning Lawrence some slight literary fame his bad health brought his career as a teacher to an end. He had pneumonia while at the school in London (he was ultimately to die of a related disease, consumption) and suffered from neuritis. From 1912 onwards he gave up working as a teacher and supported himself by his pen.

Although Lawrence left Eastwood for London in 1908 it took him years to break all those ties with his home which form the subject of *Sons and Lovers*. His mother did not die until 1910; he kept up a personal relationship with Jessie Chambers until 1912; he had other women friends in the Midlands and in London who were the originals of Clara Dawes; he frequently revisited Nottingham. Only in 1912 did the final break come. In that year he met Frieda, a German woman married to an English professor in Nottingham, with whom he soon went abroad and with whom he was to spend the rest of his life. Paul

Morel's repeated threats to go abroad at the end of *Sons and Lovers* are autobiographical. Appropriately enough Lawrence, who had begun this novel in 1910, was able to finish it, with Frieda's help, while living abroad. It was published in 1913.

Sons and Lovers is the final testament of Lawrence's background and its profound influence on him. From this point onwards his life followed a quite different pattern. Instead of the situation portrayed in the novel Lawrence's later life was characterised by his permanent relationship with Frieda, his virtual self-exile from Britain and by his status as a full-time writer. It was also marked by ill-health and, at times, by poverty.

In 1912 Lawrence went first to Germany, where he was joined by Frieda. They walked over the Alps together and settled for a time in Italy. Apart from some time spent in Germany and a few months in England, during which Frieda tried to arrange a divorce from her husband, Lawrence stayed in Italy while he wrote *The Rainbow*. His self-exile, however, was interrupted by the First World War which forced him to return to England. With a German wife he was a natural object of suspicion to the British authorities and for this, as well as for ideological reasons, the war years were a nightmare to him.

To make matters worse *The Rainbow* was declared obscene and suppressed soon after it was published in 1915; after that Lawrence had difficulty in getting his other work published in Britain. *Women in Love*, although completed in 1916, was not published until 1920 and then it appeared privately in New York.

After the war the Lawrences travelled to Italy and settled for some time in Sicily. In 1922 they started a long journey round the world during which they stopped for extensive periods in Ceylon, Australia, Mexico and the United States. During this trip, and in fact throughout this period 1918 to 1925, Lawrence wrote an immense amount including travel books, poetry, essays, short stories, history and, of course, his novels *The Lost Girl, Aaron's Rod, Kangaroo* and *The Plumed Serpent*. All of these reflect his main philosophy (which will be discussed in a later section) and the last two novels mentioned have a political theme. Lawrence had by this time become an idealist who believed in the possibility of creating a better world and his restless travelling is partly explained by his desire to observe other forms of culture which might be superior to the culture of war-torn northern Europe.

The last part of Lawrence's life was spent in Europe, however. With Frieda he spent the years 1925 to 1930 in Italy, Switzerland, Austria, Germany and France. He died in the south of France in 1930. During this period he worked hard when illness permitted and *Lady Chatterley's Lover* was only one of the many results.

Lawrence was only 45 when he died. During the last twenty years of his life he travelled and wrote about as much as was humanly possible. This gives us a clue to his personality and to his philosophy: he was an intensely energetic person and his religion was the energy and intensity of life.

Lawrence's literary and cultural background

Lawrence's life and work represent a revolt against the values and ideals of the nineteenth century. We can consider this from a social and psychological point of view and from a literary point of view.

Nineteenth-century England, the England of Queen Victoria (who reigned from 1837 to 1901) was, in Lawrence's view, unsatisfactory. He felt that the society of that period (and the values of that society persisted until at least 1914) was lifeless and artificial. The barriers between classes he found to be obstacles to real, living relationships between people. The industrialisation of Britain had produced a breed of men who were too mechanical and uniform for his taste. The Christianity which was very much the public religion of the nineteenth century was a cold religion full of prohibitions and feelings of guilt. Above all the simple passion of man and woman was not allowed to take its natural course in this rather rigid society.

All this is important to *Sons and Lovers*. There the class conflict is apparent in the relationship between Mr and Mrs Morel. The evils of industrialisation are apparent in the gloomy rows of miners' houses; and in Paul himself we see the struggles of a man emerging from a rather narrow form of Christianity and coming to terms with his own sexuality.

From a psychological point of view Lawrence's revolt against the world in which he grew up is an extreme version of the revolt of many young people against the standards of their parents. Paul Morel's dislike of his father is evident in *Sons and Lovers* and although he clearly loves his mother and needs her the novel is to a large extent the story of his escaping from her influence.

From a literary point of view Lawrence was also a rebel like his contemporaries James Joyce and, in poetry, T.S. Eliot and Ezra Pound. This generation of writers, sometimes called 'Modernist', rebelled against traditional methods of writing novels and poems. In the case of Lawrence this rebellion took various forms: he felt that the novel could become more personal and less objective; he saw the possibility that language could describe in detail the personal experiences of emotion and passion as it were 'from the inside'. His prose often feels as though it were trying to come out of the page and force the reader to agree with it and to feel as its author felt. Lawrence pours his heart and soul into his writing and is passionate and subjective in a way that was not usual in earlier fiction. Instead of the 'broad canvas' on which Dickens painted, where characters and incidents crowd together in lively confusion, Lawrence concentrates on just a few individuals and explores their souls. At the same time he feels free to express his own ideas directly to the reader, commenting on the action, teaching lessons, even preaching.

James Joyce experimented with a similar concentration on the individual and during the years when Lawrence was conceiving and writing *Sons and Lovers* Joyce was working on his novel *A Portrait of the Artist as a Young Man* (finally published in 1916). The 'Artist' in this title is Joyce himself just as Paul Morel is Lawrence himself. At the same time, in France, Marcel Proust was writing the deeply autobiographical *A la recherche du temps perdu* of which the first volume was published in the same year as *Sons and Lovers*, 1913. This subjective tendency in the novel did not stop there. Joyce went on to write a novel in what amounted to a private language (*Finnegans Wake*, 1939) while others, such as Virginia Woolf and William Faulkner, developed a technique of writing novels so subjective that they consist only of the immediate stream of thoughts passing through a character's mind. This is called the 'stream-of-consciousness' method.

Lawrence was not quite as extreme as Joyce but his work always has a personal tone and often (as in *Kangaroo* for instance) his novels are very close indeed to being unchanged accounts of his own experiences.

Another feature of Lawrence's literary background was the influence on him of the novelist and poet Thomas Hardy (1840-1928). Lawrence wrote a long critical study of Hardy but even without this evidence we would know that Hardy had influenced him. Hardy is a great novelist of the countryside and he sets his plots against an intense natural background which is not merely scenery but plays an important element in his novels. Lawrence also has a concentration on nature that is immediately obvious in *Sons and Lovers*. Moments of emotion are often preceded by a detailed description of the scene in which they are set and some of the strongest writing in the novel concerns flowers, trees, hills and the weather.

The Victorian age really came to an end with the First World War (1914-1918) and Lawrence's career developed swiftly after this world-shaking event. In a sense Lawrence was 'proved right'. His increasing rebelliousness and his increasing outspokenness on the subject of sexual relations were less unusual in the 1920s and 1930s than they would have been before the war. However, his most outspoken novel, *Lady Chatterley's Lover* (written between 1926 and 1930), was banned in Britain and in America until 1960. Thus we can see Lawrence as a pioneer of the modern novel, exploring hitherto forbidden territory and opening up a new, frank approach to life.

Lawrence as a poet

Lawrence was a very prolific writer indeed. Beside his published work (at least fifty different volumes) he wrote letters constantly to all sorts of friends and acquaintances, translated works from the Italian, and at his death left some twenty partly completed works. This is not the place to discuss this work but it is essential for the reader of *Sons and Lovers* to have some idea of Lawrence the poet.

His first complete volume of poetry was published in 1913, the same year as *Sons and Lovers*, and it was followed by nearly a dozen other volumes. His verse is direct, jerky, personal, rather 'unpoetic'. It does not have the regular rhyme and rhythm schemes of traditional verse. Lawrence preferred an irregular, almost conversational tone to the quality we associate with many of the great poets of the past. Lawrence's verse, in fact, has some of the quality of his prose and its concerns are very similar to those of the novels. In our case we can profitably look at the poems that correspond to the period of Lawrence's adolescence. In these early poems the themes of Paul Morel's development are traced in a variety of ways. One poem is even called 'Last Words to Miriam' as though Miriam were a real person.

As a poet Lawrence is interested in nature and in man's physical relationships with nature and with women. He writes of flowers and animals, of fish and insects, of moments of insight into the physical world which he always found so miraculous. There are also satirical poems and mystical religious poems which remind the reader of those elements in his novels.

It has been said that Lawrence was more of a poet in his prose than he was in his poetry. We will see this working in the analysis of *Sons and Lovers*.

The writing of *Sons and Lovers*

As early as 1910 Lawrence was working on *Sons and Lovers*. At that time it was to be called *Paul Morel* and Lawrence wrote to the publisher in October 1910 that 'about one-eighth' of it was written and that it was 'plotted out very interestingly (to me)'. That 'to me' hints at the novel's autobiographical status.

In 1912, when Lawrence had met Frieda and eloped with her to Germany, he continued writing the novel and was able to finish it by the end of the year. However, Lawrence was almost never satisfied with his work after he had written the first draft and the book which was sent to London at the end of 1912 was a much revised version of the *Paul Morel* book. As late as August 1912 he set about writing the final version, first published in 1913. This demonstrates that Lawrence, although he was beginning to break away from the more traditional and well-ordered way of writing novels, did not simply pour out his feelings in a formless mass but revised carefully.

A note on the text

Sons and Lovers, in its final version, was published in 1913 in London by Duckworth & Co.; it was the third of Lawrence's novels to appear. Since 1948 it has been available in a paperback edition published by Penguin Books. The hardback edition is published by William Heinemann.

Part 2

Summaries
of SONS AND LOVERS

A general summary

The novel is divided into two parts. In the first part Paul Morel is only one element in the story, in the second part he emerges to dominate it.

The novel opens with a description and analysis of the marriage of Paul's mother and father. Their life together in Bestwood is summarised and explained so that the reader gets a strong impression of the background against which the children are to grow up. Mrs Morel is the central figure and it is she who wins the battle with her husband. The chapter titles make this clear: 'Early married life . . . Another battle . . . Casting off of Morel.' The third chapter is in fact entitled 'The casting off of Morel—The taking on of William'. This 'casting off' and 'taking on' are done by Mrs Morel who, deciding that her husband is no good, turns to her eldest son, William, and gives him the affection and interest that could have been his father's.

Paul comes on the scene first as a baby, then as a schoolboy, and very much as a second son. His mother is proud of him and helps him to develop intellectually and to get his first job, but her chief love is William. William goes away to London, which upsets Mrs Morel, and there meets a pretty but shallow girl whom he brings home to Bestwood for some rather awkward visits. Quite suddenly William develops pneumonia in London and dies, to his mother's great grief. After a period of emotional withdrawal she begins to turn her affections towards Paul.

Thus in the first part of the novel (Chapters 1 to 6) we have been given all the information necessary for an understanding of the main interest of the second part, which is twice as long. This main interest is the development, emotional and intellectual, of Paul. In the first part there has really been very little *story*. We have seen Mr and Mrs Morel moving house and we have witnessed William's emergence from home; we have also seen his death and Paul's first steps in the big world. None of this 'story' is as significant as the emotional conflicts and developments which have taken place. Lawrence is really concerned with the battle between man and woman (Mr and Mrs Morel) and with the inability of William to find a satisfactory woman because he is under his mother's influence. We have also been given a clear picture of the things which are important to young Paul: the fascination and horror of the mine where his father works, the disturbance of his parents' quarrels, the jealousy he feels of his mother, his reactions to work.

If the novel were *primarily* about Mrs Morel it would not be divided into two parts. From her point of view there are three phases: her husband, William, and Paul. But the novel is primarily about Paul so there are only two phases: his early life when his mother is concerned mainly with her husband or William, and his adolescence when she is concerned with him.

Thus the second part of *Sons and Lovers* (Chapters 7 to 15) traces the development of Paul against the background established in the first part. Paul is present on nearly every page of the nine chapters of this part. Again, there is not very much actual *story*. Paul works in Jordan's factory throughout Part Two of the novel and although he is obviously promoted during this time this is hardly mentioned. His successes as a painter are mentioned rather more often but in both these cases Lawrence's interest is clearly not in Paul's job or his painting for their own sakes. The job is only mentioned when it is necessary to explain his relationship with Clara, who also works at Jordan's, and the painting is only mentioned when it is necessary to establish Mrs Morel's attitude towards her son's achievements.

Instead of being a 'story', then, Part Two of *Sons and Lovers* is a study of emotion. Everything in the novel takes second place to the emotional conflicts and in Part Two this means the conflict for Paul's soul fought by his mother, Miriam and Clara. His mother is suspicious of Miriam because she sees that Miriam wants to have the whole of Paul to herself and will leave none of him for her. Paul loves Miriam at first but, as he grows up, he begins to realise that their relationship is too much a matter of the mind and not enough of the body; when they eventually become lovers it is not a success because Miriam does not actually want Paul as a man although she adores him in every other respect. Paul does not even really want Miriam: their relationship has been too spiritual. Against this is set Clara who, although physically luxuriant, has a passive, animal-like mental calmness. She is not stupid but she is a woman of a large, slow, accepting, physical type which in Lawrence symbolises the wisdom of the flesh rather at the expense of the spirit.

Paul's mother dies. He rejects Miriam and he finally encourages Clara to return to her husband, Baxter Dawes. At the end of the novel there is no woman left to hold him in Nottingham and he talks of going abroad. This must be symbolic. The ties of his childhood are broken and he is an adult who can now leave the home in which he was born and brought up.

The title

The novel was originally called *Paul Morel*, which reflects its main interest accurately. Its final title, *Sons and Lovers*, reflects both this main interest (Paul himself) and its secondary theme as well. William, Paul (and, to a small extent, Arthur), the sons of Mrs Morel, are taken by her as 'lovers' (not in the physical sense) when she has 'cast off' her husband. They are thus her 'sons and lovers'. Paul, of course, is a son and also the lover of Miriam and Clara. The final title emphasises Paul's relationship both to his mother and to the other women.

Detailed summaries: Part one

Chapter 1: The early married life of the Morels

Lawrence opens his novel with a detailed geographical and historical introduction to Bestwood. Only in the eighth paragraph does he introduce Mrs Morel who is mentioned as having two children, and as expecting a third. These children appear in their excitement to go to the fair while her husband is kept in the background. At first he only gets one brief sentence, 'Her husband was a miner'. Later, when Mrs Morel is at the fair with Annie, Morel is mentioned as having been seen in a pub; he is obviously going to be a secondary character.

Mrs Morel's dissatisfaction with her husband is made clear. She walks outside, feeling hot and heavy in her pregnancy, then goes in again to wait for Morel. He comes in drunk. Now that we have met him Lawrence gives us the details of his past with Mrs Morel: their meeting, their mutual attraction, their marriage, her gradual discovery that he was irresponsible and that he could not manage money. Some of their arguments are described and Lawrence brings us back to the 'present' of the novel in the paragraph opening 'At the wakes time . . .'

Once we are back in the present, now equipped with most of the information we need to understand the situation, we are given a lengthy account of one particular day of battle between husband and wife. Morel and his 'pal' (friend) Jerry Purdy spend a day walking to Nottingham where they enjoy themselves and drink plenty of beer. When Morel returns home he is drunk, depressed and bad-tempered. They have a serious quarrel and Morel locks his wife out of the house; at last he lets her in and the chapter ends with him in drunken sleep.

NOTES:
1. **'The Bottoms' succeeded to 'Hell Row'.** In this opening sentence Lawrence sets the tone of his description of the Bestwood mining community. With street-names such as these we are unlikely to find much elegance or optimism here.

2. **The houses themselves were substantial and very decent.** In this paragraph the repetition of the word 'little' suggests a sort of meanness in the lives of the miners.

3. **She despised him and was tied to him.** A strongly-worded summary of Mrs Morel's relationship with her husband.

4. **Oh! Oh! waitin' for me, lass?** In this conversation, and throughout the rest of the book, Morel speaks in a Midland dialect. Sometimes the other characters do the same, but generally Mrs Morel and her children are shown to be more refined by speaking normal English. Morel omits certain letters, especially the letter 'h' at the beginning of words, the letter 'g' at the end of words and the last letter of some short words. Thus:

waitin'	=	waiting	th'	=	the
'elpin'	=	helping	o'	=	of
an'	=	and		

Besides this he shortens some words, thus:

gen	=	given	gi'ein'	=	giving
b'ra	=	but a		

He also uses certain dialect words, thus:

nowt	=	nothing	mucky	=	dirty

In addition to this his dialect employs the second person singular ('thee', 'thy' and 'thou') when talking to family and close friends. This habit, which has now died out almost completely in England, is the equivalent of the French 'tu' and the German 'du'. It simply means 'you'. Thus:

I browt thee = I brought you

tha niver said (thou never said) = you never said

thy life = your life

Arena ter (Aren't thou) = Aren't you

Tha'd better (Thou had better) = You had better

Later in this chapter we learn that one of the things that attracted Mrs Morel to Morel in the first place was this odd form of speech which clearly made her feel intimate with the speaker:

'Should ter like it?' he asked tenderly. 'Appen not, it 'ud dirty thee'.
She had never been 'thee'd' and 'thou'd' before.
The next Christmas they were married.

Finally, Lawrence spells some ordinary English words in an unusual way to show how they should be pronounced, as in 'browt' (='brought') and 'niver' (='never') above. Thus:

hae'f-crown	=	half-crown (piece of money)
ivry	=	every
thank yer	=	thank you

It is not essential for the student of *Sons and Lovers* to understand every detail of this dialect; usually it is possible to get a general idea of what Morel is saying without translating every word. However, in these notes an explanation is given of all the more difficult pieces of dialect.

5. **Congregationalism.** This is a minor, puritan Christian sect. Congregationalists, like Methodists and many others, are Protestant Christians whose practices are somewhat stricter and simpler than those of the main English Protestant Church, the Anglican Church. Anglicans go to *church* while Congregationalists and similar go to *chapel*. Congregationalism has found most of its followers in towns. Here Mrs Morel's family is shown as being slightly socially superior to that of Morel in that he is a largely pagan miner while she comes from the rather narrow but proud 'burgher' (i.e. urban) class (shopkeepers and the like) which supported the puritan Oliver Cromwell (one of whose officers was the Colonel Hutchinson here mentioned) against the Anglican King Charles I during the Civil War (1642–9).

6. **'This act of masculine clumsiness was the spear through the side of her love for Morel'.** Notice the reference here to Christ who, after dying on the cross, had a spear put into his side. (See the account in the Gospel of St John, 19:33).

7. **'She became aware of something about her'.** Here Mrs Morel is out in her garden and she has an intense experience with the white lilies in the moonlight. This is the first of several places in the novel where an emotional moment is associated with an intense experience of nature.

GLOSSARY:
Note: see note 4, *above, about the Midland dialect employed in parts of the novel.*

'appen:	it may happen that
bezzle:	to drink
butty:	senior miner
clunch:	lump, presumably of coal
favour:	to resemble
moudiwarp:	mole
wakes:	an annual fair

Chapter 2: The birth of Paul, and another battle

This chapter opens with a loving description of Morel's preparations for work which is followed, after a brief exchange between husband and wife, by a description of the life of Mrs Morel while she is pregnant with Paul. Her life is not described directly but we get a fair impression of it from the talk she has with her neighbour and the preparations that are made for her confinement. Then we are with Morel again and we see him at work down the pit.

Paul is born and we see his mother's reaction to this event (she is sick but proud) and his father's (he is bewildered). A minor character is introduced in the shape of the Congregational minister who visits Mrs Morel and is obviously a strong contrast to Morel. A further impression is given of the tension between husband and wife.

Paul's first personal appearance in the novel is in this chapter. His mother walks out into the country with him as a small baby and has a series of intense feelings connected with him—grief, guilt and love. She decides to call him Paul and from this moment onwards we know that her relationship with him will be at the centre of the novel.'

This chapter, like the first one, ends with a violent argument between the Morels. Morel is drunk again and, in their 'battle' he throws a drawer at his wife and hurts her. He is immediately sorry for what he has done and spends two days in bed. The he spends some time with his friends in the pub and, after an argument with his wife about money, threatens to leave her and actually walks out of the house with that apparent intention. He returns the same night and we can see by the end of the chapter that Mrs Morel no longer has any respect for him; all she feels is contempt and bitterness.

NOTES:
1. **He went downstairs in his shirt.** In this and the following paragraphs we can see Lawrence's delight in physical details and his capacity for describing daily routines vividly.

2. **Tuppence-ha'penny.** 'Tuppence' means 'two pence' or 'two pennies'. A ha'penny is a half penny. Even in the period referred to (1880s–90s) this was not much money, being approximately 1 per cent of £1.

3. **Morel was not as a rule . . .** In these pages Lawrence's interest in the business of mining is obvious. It has been said that the frequent references to darkness in his work came from his childhood fear and wonder at his father's dark job.

4. **You might fetch Mrs Bower.** Mrs Bower is the local midwife. Probably she is without medical qualifications but has long experience.

5. **The wedding at Cana.** This refers to the wedding-feast at the village of Cana mentioned in the Bible where Christ reportedly performed his first miracle. The wine having run out at the feast, he changed water into wine to make up the deficiency. It is appropriate here because, of course, we are considering the Morels' marriage. (See John, 2.)

6. The Holy Ghost. Most Christians believe that God has three 'persons': Father (Jehovah), Son (Christ) and Holy Ghost.

7. Perhaps her son would be a Joseph. Joseph, son of Jacob, is a character from the Bible (Old Testament). His story can be read in the Book of Genesis, 37–50. The point of the allusion to him here is that he rose to power and wealth unexpectedly in a way that Mrs Morel imagines may happen to Paul.

GLOSSARY:

barkled:	thirsty
canna:	cannot
dingin':	hitting, banging
gabeys:	idiots
grange:	barn
lass:	girl
loose-all:	the signal given at the mine to indicate the end of the working day
owt:	anything
peg:	(*here*) leg
sluther:	slithering; (*here*) noise of boots on the ground
wagging:	(*here*) carrying on

Chapter 3: The casting off of Morel—The taking on of William

Morel becomes ill and the early pages of this chapter describe how the illness brings the 'separating parents' back together temporarily. The period of domestic peace results in a fourth child—Arthur. The Morel children, in order of age, are: William, Annie, Paul and Arthur.

The peace is broken by a fierce quarrel when Morel wants, unreasonably, to beat William for fighting with a neighbour's boy. After this episode Lawrence describes Mrs Morel's attempts at self-education and her efforts to make William something better than a miner. The rest of the chapter revolves round her relationship with William and his development. Like Paul later in the novel William gets a job in Nottingham and starts to take an interest in girls. This is a source of pride and jealousy to the mother. She wants to see William succeed in the great world but she does not want to lose this son, who is also her 'lover', to another woman. (See p.14).

Various incidents are recounted to make this relationship clear. Mrs Morel does not like William to go to dances (she herself met Morel at a dance) and turns his girl-friends away from the door rudely when they come to visit him. She behaves like a jealous lover when he goes out to a fancy-dress ball and does not even stay at home to see him dressed up.

It is clear in this chapter that Morel has lost the battle with his wife. In the arguments he has with her about William (concerning punishment or whether he should become a miner) she wins. From this point onwards he fades into the background of the novel. Thus the first part of the title of the chapter is accurate—Morel is 'cast off'. As to the other part, it is not entirely true to say that William is 'taken on'; certainly his mother tries to take him on, and to some extent she succeeds, but he is obviously keen to escape from the nest and make his own life with his own choice of women. Before the end of the chapter he has been offered, and has accepted, a job in London. His mother is sad; we see them together burning his old love-letters and here Mrs Morel is able to come between him and his girl-friends for the last time.

NOTES:

1. **So Mrs Morel bought him elixir of vitriol.** In this paragraph and the next are given the names of several old-fashioned or home-made medicines and of the herbs that go into them. It is hardly necessary to understand exactly what each of them is; it is, however, important to get the general impression that Morel, and his fellow-miners, take a childish delight in these old country remedies which may not really be very effective.

2. **Clubs.** Before the days of proper insurances against illness working people used to form 'clubs' into which they paid a small amount each week. Then, when for some reason one member of the club could not work, there was money to support him and his family.

3. **A cobbler 'as 'ad licked seventeen.** A 'cobbler' here means a 'conker' or horse-chestnut, a hard inedible nut which boys sometimes put on strings. They can then play a game in which one boy uses his 'conker' on a string to hit the other boy's 'conker'. After a number of hits, which the boys take in turn, one of the nuts gets broken and the other is said to have won. 'Licked' here is a slang word for 'beaten'. So the phrase refers to a horse-chestnut which has beaten seventeen others at the game, as is explained a few lines further on.

4. **The Co-operative Wholesale Society.** The 'Co-op' is an organisation, started in the industrial parts of England in the nineteenth century, that carries out wholesale and retail trade but gives the profit back to the members—that is, to those who buy from the Co-op itself.

5. **A Highlander.** A man from the North of Scotland. The dress referred to would include a kilt and be made of tartan.

6. **Transpires.** Mrs Morel, in her eagerness to be nasty about William's girls, misunderstands this word and seems to associate it with 'perspires' (= 'sweats').

GLOSSARY:

barm-man:	man selling 'barm', i.e. yeast for the making of bread
britches:	breeches; trousers
errant swain:	a joking reference to romantic love-tales in which this sort of language is used. The words mean a lover who is 'errant' because he is not paying his girl the attention he should
fancy-dress ball:	a dance for which everybody dresses up in clothing typical of some country or famous character or historical period
flame:	(*here*) lover; girl- or boy-friend
mardy:	weak; soft
mater:	mother—a rather educated and even upper-class word; 'mater' is the Latin for 'mother'
peens:	pains
shonna I?:	shan't I? (= Shall not I?)
snipey:	unpleasant; rude; bitchy
stool-harsed Jack:	man who sits on a stool to work; clerk

Chapter 4: The young life of Paul

This chapter does not deal with Paul's boyhood in strict order. It gives us a number of marvellous sketches of what that boyhood was like at different times. The characters are the same as in the earlier chapters but Paul now dominates the scene with only his mother as a rival.

We witness the 'sacrifice' of Annie's doll when Paul burns it; then we see his father and William fighting over Mrs Morel (it is clear here that we have moved back in time to before the end of Chapter 3 when William went to London). Next Lawrence describes what it was like for the children when their parents moved to the house up on the hill: the sound of the wind in a nearby tree is presented in detail and we get an insight into the children's minds. Details are then given of Paul's struggle to keep his mother's attention and of his jealousy of his father. In fact, Morel can be friendly and nice to his children, as in the episode where he tells little Arthur about the pit-pony or in the descriptions of his work in the house when he mends things. But in general he is bad-tempered and dangerous and Lawrence gives us a strong sense of the children's fear and hate of him.

Paul becomes ill and all the associations of the illness (the attentions of his mother, the happiness when he starts to get better) are very carefully presented. Even more ordinary domestic happenings are handled with love and detail: shopping, collecting mushrooms. There is a long and vivid description of Paul's embarrassment when he goes to collect

his father's wages; it is a masterpiece of perception into the boy's feelings and shows Lawrence at his best as a writer of dialogue. Then there
is a description of Paul's happiness when he is alone with his mother
and sharing her delight in pretty china and flowers.

Perhaps moving backwards in time, Lawrence now offers a picture
of Paul and his brother, sister and friends playing games outdoors.
Next he describes the irritation and unhappiness caused in the summer
months when the miners leave work early and there is less money.
The chapter ends with the excitement of William's return home for
Christmas.

Lawrence's unusual method, in this chapter and in the whole book,
of presenting things from different moments of time all together will
be discussed in Part 3 of these notes.

NOTES:
1. **Let's make a sacrifice of Arabella.** The young Paul is upset and guilty
   because he has destroyed his sister's doll but his reaction is both
   religious and sadistic—he wants to burn it. Perhaps this connects
   with his relationships with Miriam and Clara.
2. **But the best time for the young children was when he made fuses.**
   'Fuses' are small tubes of inflammable material (here straws filled
   with gunpowder) which are used to ignite explosives in the mine.
   Morel has an old-fashioned way of making them.
3. **Well, there's one little 'oss.** This ''oss' (horse) is a pit-pony. Ponies
   were used in the mines (pits) to pull the coal-wagons until about 1920.
4. **The Midland.** Until the nationalisation of the railways, after the
   Second World War (1948), different parts of Britain were served by
   four main companies, which were made from the grouping (in 1923)
   of different, private railway companies. Nottingham was served in
   1913 by the Midland Railway, later part of the London, Midland and
   Scottish company.

GLOSSARY:

bacca:	tobacco
bad un:	bad one; bad person
bested:	beat, in the sense of 'arrived first'
brakes:	(*here*) horse-drawn vans
cadin':	in a friendly way
chelp:	cheek; impudence
de haut en bas:	(*French*) from top to bottom
duckey:	term of endearment
fawce:	clever; cunning
flamin':	adjective indicating annoyance, like 'bloody'
flybie-skybie:	a home-made description of Annie denoting her wild ways as a child

frumenty:	a dish made of wheat, hot milk and sugar
holled:	thrown
impidence:	impudence; rudeness
jockey:	(*here*) lad
jowl:	knock; punch
kissing-bunch:	bunch of mistletoe, a traditional Christmas decoration under which anybody may claim a kiss
knocked-off:	finished work
lerky:	a children's game
nubbly:	lumpy
oddwares:	all sorts of things; the 'oddwares man' would sell toys, ironmongery, anything
'oss:	horse
penn'orth:	penny-worth
scrattlin':	scratching, here in the sense of 'poor'
scotch:	(*here*) interruption
slives (slivin'):	slips; slides (slippery)
snap:	snack; something to eat
snied:	full
stall:	subdivision of the coal-mine
stew-jack:	stew; meat dish
tomboy:	girl who acts boyishly
whoam:	home
y'ead:	your head

Chapter 5: Paul launches into life

Morel breaks his leg badly in the mine and the family are anxious, but Paul enjoys being 'the man of the house' in his father's absence. Mother and father are brought a little closer together by the accident but it is clear now that she no longer loves him.

Paul is now fourteen and has to leave school. We are given a strong impression of his shyness when he starts to look for work, then Lawrence breaks off his account of Paul's development briefly to tell us about William and his involvement with an obviously unsuitable young woman. Then we are back with Paul again for the rest of the chapter.

He goes to Nottingham with his mother to be interviewed for a job as a clerk at Jordan's factory where such things as wooden legs and thick stockings (clothes with a medical purpose; 'surgical appliances') are made. We witness the interview with Mr Jordan, and Paul's shame and embarrassment, but he gets the job and starts work almost at once. Lawrence is careful to provide the reader with many of the details of Paul's new life and the background of poverty and hard work in which his mother survives.

Then, in a vivid and effective passage, Paul's first day at Jordan's is described (Lawrence catches the feelings of a boy plunged into a strange world very well. He meets the different groups of workers in the factory and learns the long routine of every day. He returns home to his anxious mother. In the remaining pages of the chapter Lawrence describes different aspects of Paul's continuing life at Jordan's.

NOTES:

1. **And those granite setts at Tinder Hill.** 'Setts' are cobbles, paving-stones on the road. Here Mrs Morel is thinking of some badly-laid 'setts' which make the road rough. With his broken leg, and in a badly sprung horse-drawn cart, Morel will suffer as he is driven over them.

2. **Already he was a prisoner of industrialism.** This may be a small joke at Paul's expense, but the rest of this paragraph makes it clear that Lawrence is quite conventional in the way he sets the slavery of the industrial world against the freedom of nature.

3. **The elder brother was becoming quite swanky.** 'Swanky' here means 'upper-class', 'snobby'. The paragraph ends with the magic word 'gentleman'. Of course William is *not* a gentleman: his background, education and employment in London associate him first with the working class and then with the lower-middle class. But he is taking on some of the airs of a gentleman, and he insists that his girl-friend is 'a lady'.

4. **And they ventured under the archway.** We notice in this paragraph a concentration on dark, dirty, ominous images and adjectives. We get an intense impression of young Paul's fear and revulsion.

5. **It was a note in French.** Paul's French is correct. *'Gris fil bas'* means 'grey thread stockings'; *'sans doigts'* means 'without fingers' or, here, 'toes'.

6. **Mr J.A. Bates, Esquire.** In written addresses 'Mr', traditionally, is for those who are not gentlemen; 'Esquire' is for those who are. It is wrong to write both.

7. **Elaine in 'Idylls of the King'.** One of several beautiful women in Lord Tennyson's poems about King Arthur and his court (published 1859).

8. **'Arabian Nights'.** The famous collection of Arab folk-tales published in Arabic under the title *Alf Lila Wa Lila* (*A Thousand Nights and a Night*) supposedly told by the Princess Sheharazad to her master, the Caliph of Baghdad, night after night in order to save her life.

GLOSSARY:

a month of Sundays:	a long time
au revoy:	(*from the French, au revoir*) good-bye
boss:	(*here*) projecting wooden object; part of the girls' equipment for making stockings
brazen hussy:	a pejorative phrase for an over-self-confident young woman
buck up:	hurry up
clod:	(*here*) fool
draggled:	brought down into poverty and squalor
dunna ax me:	don't ask me
hank:	coil of thread
I'd 'a eaten 'em:	I would have eaten them (i.e. I would have done them more quickly)
lout:	badly behaved young man
Norfolk suit:	typical child's suit of the period
prime:	(*here*) good
robinet:	(*French*) literally a 'tap'
saloon bar:	part of a 'pub'; drinking establishment
setts:	paving-stones
spiral:	(*here*) connected with the machinery used for making elastic, a major part of Jordan's business
swanky:	snobbish; glamorous
tripping:	(*here*) walking quickly
trusses:	surgical appliances made of elastic, worn round the stomach
Yorkshire terrier:	breed of small dog

Chapter 6: Death in the family

This chapter, which brings Part One of the novel to an end, deals with William. It is necessary at this stage for Lawrence to finish with William and to establish Paul as the central interest. Morel is by now a weak character but Mrs Morel still loves William. Arthur does not seem to be a competitor for her love and Annie, besides being a girl, is very much a background figure. Before we can concentrate fully on Paul we must see how Mrs Morel's love is taken from William and given to him.

William brings home his fiancée, who is sometimes called 'Gyp' (short for 'Gipsy') and sometimes Lily. She calls William 'Chubby'. She is a hopelessly inadequate, selfish, empty-headed creature whose only interest seems to be in clothes and the small details of social life. William fully understands her inadequacy but seems to be powerless to break the spell she has cast over him. Their visit to Bestwood is brilliantly described. The tensions in the house are numerous: Morel admires Lily but Mrs Morel does not; Paul adores her and Mrs Morel is jealous of this; William is sometimes proud of her and sometimes hates her.

The central issue seems to be whether William is really capable of forming a good relationship with a sensible woman or whether, because of his close tie with his mother, he is forced to stick to empty women like Lily who are no threat to his mother's love for him.

There is a long section in the middle of the chapter, between the two parts dealing with William, which describes Paul's first visit, with his mother, to Willey Farm, the home of Miriam Leivers and her family. Mother and son are almost like lovers in their excitement as they walk to the farm and spend the afternoon there. Paul, aged sixteen, meets Miriam, who is fourteen, but the day is a high point in his relationship with his mother. 'The mother and son were in ecstasy together'.

William comes home again and complains even more rudely about Lily. He hates her at times but he seems to be trapped by her. He returns to London and there he becomes ill and dies of pneumonia. Morel is shattered by the news, and makes him retreat from life yet further. Mrs Morel is almost killed by her son's death. For three months she sits and does nothing; then Paul becomes ill too and has a dangerous attack of pneumonia. This brings his mother out of her depression and from this point he is her main source of pride and joy.

NOTES:

1. **And his father . . .** In this paragraph Lawrence employs one of his favourite devices—repetition. The word 'mean' comes to be strongly associated with Morel.

2. **Grammar School . . . Board-School.** Schools for 12–18-year-olds and 5–12-year-olds respectively. Britain now has comprehensive schools (12–18) and primary schools (5–12) as well as other types of school.

3. **Realise.** Lawrence uses this verb in a special way to mean 'fully understand', 'feel with' and 'recognise as a full human being'.

4. **The Lady of the Lake.** A mocking reference to Miriam's taste for romantic stories: she imagines herself to be somebody from the Arthurian legends.

5. **She has been confirmed three times.** During adolescence most Christians are expected to 'confirm' the vows made for them at baptism. It is a ceremony, performed by a Bishop, during which the young person would, temporarily, be at the centre of attention.

6. **Elmer's End . . . King's Cross . . . Cannon Street.** Lawrence seems to have invented the London suburb of Elmer's End where William lives. The other two names refer to railway stations in London.

GLOSSARY:

blessed:	(*here*) ironic version of 'damned', a swear-word
bobby-dazzler:	something or someone glamorous or impressive
cheer:	(*here*) chair
chlorodyne gum:	chewing-gum
Christmas-box:	Christmas-present of money
duffer:	fool
foulard:	type of silk
gen:	given
gilliver:	a flower (different types of flowers have this name; also called 'gilly flower')
heliotrope:	a flower (*Heliotropium*)
heron:	a bird
mardy-kid:	weak child
marrons glacés:	(*French*) crystallised chestnuts (sweets)
peaked:	(*here*) white with nervousness
peewit:	a bird, also called lapwing
poitry:	poetry
rake:	(*here*) playboy; waster
show:	(*here*) life; opportunity
sprig:	(*here*) pattern; decorate
suède:	soft leather
tha's let on me:	you have got here before me
winder:	something that takes one's breath away, a surprise

Part two

Chapter 7: Lad-and-girl love

As its title implies, this chapter concentrates on the first stages of Paul's relationship with Miriam. During the chapter we see various aspects of their life together while Paul is between the ages of about sixteen and about nineteen.

First they are together at Willey Farm. Paul becomes a favourite with the Leivers family and through them comes to experience life close to nature. Mrs Leivers offers an interesting contrast to Mrs Morel and it is significant that Paul seems at one point to have a closer relationship with her than with Miriam. But the main force of Lawrence's writing is towards explaining Miriam's character and the effect she and Paul have on each other.

At first they play together like children. Then we see them studying together, Paul teaching Miriam algebra and French with a mixture of patience and bad temper. Miriam adores Paul for his supposed intellectuality. Their relationship is concerned with books, flowers and going to chapel. Two walks are described when, with friends, Paul and Miriam visit the Hemlock Stone and Wingfield Manor. These are opportunities for Paul to show his developing interest in the world and in Miriam; she, on the other hand, reveals herself as cut-off and painfully shy.

Mrs Morel does not like Miriam but the Morel family and Miriam go together for a holiday to the seaside. Paul is uncertain about his girl-friend and hardly knows whether she irritates him or whether he loves her. A huge barrier of 'purity' is between them and it seems impossible that they will ever be able to love physically: towards the end of the chapter they prove to be unable even to kiss one another.

NOTES:

1. **A Walter Scott heroine.** Sir Walter Scott (1771-1832) was a Romantic novelist; in his novels (largely historical) the heroes and heroines have vices and virtues which are sometimes rather exaggerated.

2. **Christ and God made one great figure.** Miriam's theology is not really odd here. To most Christians Christ and God are separate but identical, whence the 'Father and Son' image.

3. **Ediths, and Lucys, and Rowenas . . .** A list of Sir Walter Scott's heroines and heroes.

4. **Colomba.** A short story by the French author Prosper Mérimée (1803-1870).

5. **Voyage autour de ma chambre.** A novel by the French author Xavier de Maistre (1763-1852).

6. **Skegness.** A seaside resort on the Lincolnshire coast.

7. **King Cophetua's beggar-maid.** King Cophetua was a legendary African king. He fell in love with a beggar girl.

8. **There's God's burning bush for you.** In one of his many appearances to Moses God took the form of a burning bush; the flames did not consume the bush.

9. **One of Reynolds's 'Choir of Angels'.** That is, like one of the angels in the picture mentioned; painted by Sir Joshua Reynolds (1723-92).

10. **Communion.** Lawrence is referring to the Christian sacrament of Communion. This is a ceremony at which Christians share bread and wine in memory of Christ's death.

11. **The Pennine Chain.** The central range of hills that run north-south down the middle of England.

12. The Flying Scotchman. Actually 'the Flying Scotsman'; a famous fast train that used to run between London and Edinburgh.

13. Annunciation. In the Christian story the 'Annunciation' is the moment when an angel appears to Mary, Christ's mother, and tells her that she is pregnant with the Son of God. Miriam is here being compared with Mary.

14. And this conversation remained graven on her mind as one of the letters of the law. The word 'graven' is old-fashioned and biblical; it makes us think of 'the law' which God gave to Moses 'graven' upon stones (see the Book of Exodus, 20-1).

15. Communion-rail. A rail in a church, where the sacrament is taken. It separates the altar from the part where the people sit.

16. Mary Queen of Scots. The most famous (and most romantic) monarch of Scottish history. She lived between 1542 and 1587 and spent the last nineteen years of her life imprisoned in England.

17. Veronese's 'St Catherine'. This is a picture painted by the Italian painter Veronese (1528-1588).

18. But there was a serpent in her Eden. Refers to the Bible (the Book of Genesis) in which Adam and Eve are tempted by the devil in the form of a snake and thus lose their earthly paradise, Eden.

19. A platonic friendship. A friendship without sexuality. Named after the Greek philosopher Plato (427-348BC).

20. Some sad Botticelli angel. Sandro Botticelli was an Italian painter (1445-1510).

GLOSSARY:

celandine:	a flower (*Ranunculus ficaria*)
coon:	(*here*) popular singer
crypt:	the cellar beneath a church
fallow:	land normally used for crops, on which nothing is being grown for a period to allow its natural level of fertility to be restored
float:	(*here*) wagon for carrying milk
fry:	(*here*) baby fish; thus: people of no importance
Good Friday:	the Friday before Easter Sunday
gumption:	intelligence and energy
in high feather:	self-confident and proud
jangle:	ugly noise; lack of harmony
Jenny wren:	small bird
kested:	(*here*) beaten

knoll:	small hill
les derniers fils d'une race épuisée:	(*French*) the last children of an exhausted race
rosary:	string of beads to assist with the saying of prayers
ripping:	(*here*) excellent
Scylla:	a flower (*Scylla* is the Latin name)
shimmer:	to shine and to flicker
shut-knives:	pen-knives
sloe-bush:	a fruit-bearing thorn bush (*Prunus spinosa*)
sorrel-heads:	the tops of a weed which grows among grass
spoon:	(*here*) kiss and cuddle
swathe:	wrap up in bandages
swine-girl:	poor girl who looks after pigs
stifle:	asphyxiate; suffocate
sugar-bag:	blue paper (traditionally used to wrap sugar)
tam-o'-shanter:	a Scottish hat
trash:	rubbish

Chapter 8: Strife in love

Arthur Morel becomes a soldier, to his parents' annoyance. Paul's paintings win prizes in an exhibition in Nottingham. Paul meets Clara and we are told about Baxter Dawes, who works at Jordan's. The rest of the chapter is devoted to Paul's relationship with Miriam and with his mother. Paul is twenty-one and Miriam twenty. His irritation with Miriam increases but he is obviously not wholly satisfied with simply loving his mother. We see him at Willey Farm and then at his own home with Miriam. Lawrence gives a marvellous description of Morel washing and drying himself and of the visit of his fellow miners to the house to share out the week's money. Morel goes to the pub and his wife to the market.

Miriam arrives and her evening with Paul is presented as a model of their whole relationship: they read and study together quite happily, but there is something unsatisfactory about their relationship. Paul is teased by a local girl, Beatrice, who visits the house briefly, and we see a contrast between Miriam and Beatrice. He allows the bread he is baking to burn, which annoys his mother when she returns; she thinks that Paul is so interested in Miriam that he cannot even concentrate on the baking.

Paul and his mother argue about Miriam when she has been taken home but they are reconciled. When Morel comes in, drunk, he nearly fights with Paul and it seems that Mrs Morel cares only for her son, not her husband, while Paul decides that his mother is more important than Miriam.

NOTES:

1. **I have taken the King's shilling.** Arthur has joined the army. The traditional way of doing this was to accept a shilling (an old piece of money) as the first part of a soldier's pay.

2. **Women's Rights.** Lawrence gives these words capital letters to show that Clara has joined what was a militant feminist movement. From the 1880s onwards there was a growing movement in Britain in favour, for example, of women being given the vote.

3. **Orion.** A constellation; a group of stars.

4. **Michelangelo.** Michelangelo, one of the great painters of the Italian Renaissance, (1475-1564).

5. **Balzac.** French novelist, Honoré de Balzac (1799-1850).

6. **Doomsday.** The last day of the world; judgement day.

7. **Liberty's.** A large shop in London specialising in fabrics.

8. **Postle.** Beatrice jokingly calls Paul 'Apostle', i.e. the Apostle Paul, follower of Christ and earnest teacher.

9. **King Alfred burned the cakes.** King Alfred (849-901) of Wessex, at a low point in his fortunes, took employment from a peasant-woman and did such small jobs for her as watching cakes while they were cooking. Naturally his mind, like Paul's here, was on other things and he let the cakes burn.

10. **He's gone off with number nine.** Leonard is here referring jokingly to the number of girl-friends Paul is thought to have.

11. **Solomon's baby.** Solomon, who has come to symbolise wisdom, was a king of the Jews. His famous judgement between two women each claiming a baby, in which he suggested that it should be divided, can be found in the Bible (First Book of Kings, 3).

12. **Baudelaire's Le Balcon.** A poem by the French poet Charles Baudelaire (1821-1867).

13. **Verlaine.** The French poet Paul Verlaine (1844-1896).

14. **Behold her singing in the field.** Part of a poem by William Wordsworth (1770-1850).

15. **Fair Ines.** A poem by Thomas Hood (1799-1845).

16. **It is a beauteous evening.** Part of another poem by Wordsworth.

17. **Tu te rappelleras . . .** Part of the poem 'Le Balcon' referred to above.

18. **Herbert Spencer.** British philosopher (1820-1903).

GLOSSARY:

agate:	going, i.e. happening
Beat:	(*here*) short form of 'Beatrice'
blubbered:	cried
boxed his ears:	hit him about the head
cavilled:	argued
ce matin etc.:	(*French*). 'This morning the birds woke me up. It was still only half light. But the little window of my room was pale, and then yellow, and all the birds of the woods burst into a lively and resounding song. The whole dawn shook. I had dreamt of you. Do you, too, see the dawn? The birds wake me up almost every morning and there is always something of terror in the noise of the thrushes. It is so clear.'
clap thysen:	put yourself
club:	it is Morel's 'club' because this week it is his turn to receive some of the money paid in weekly by all miners (see note 2 to Chapter 3).
cowd:	cold
dayman:	mine worker who is not a partner with the others but is paid by them
doo-er:	door
dunno:	do not know
every whit:	completely
go thy ways:	come on
guttle:	drink (or eat) greedily; guzzle
headstocks:	part of the equipment of the coal mine
hectoring:	bullying verbally
hug:	(*here*) carry
hurtle:	(*here*) huddle; squash into a small space
I'd as lief:	I would be as happy to . . .

if tha doesna tha durs 'na: if you do not do it, it is because you dare not
I'm come be'out the market-bag: I have come without the shopping-bag
I'm nobbut a sack of faggots: I am nothing but a sack of sticks (i.e. bones)

inter alia:	among other things
'issen:	himself
leading:	(*here*) vein of coal
measly:	mean; limited
nesh:	weak

nowt b'r a ice-'ouse: nothing but an ice-house
panchion (or punchion): large ceramic bowl

pew:	bench in church or chapel
portière:	door-curtain

salamander: a lizard-like creature supposed to be able to live in fire

sateen: shiny material

scored: (*here*) cut in several places

scrapes: (*here*) difficulties

scrattlin':   mean

sludge: mud

sops: weak or childish boys

'strewth: God's truth (*swear-word*)

swell: (*here*) grand; fashionable

tha's made thy heels crack: you have got here quickly

three hap'orth of pap: here this implies that Baxter considers Paul a valueless child

trapesing: walking wearily

tu te rappelleras la beauté des caresses: (*French*) you will remember the beauty of (our) embraces

wesh: wash

whittle: (*here*) whine; complain

Chapter 9: Defeat of Miriam

We now see Paul visiting Miriam during an Easter holiday and the first pages of this chapter are devoted to explaining their feelings for one another and to showing them together. Paul is frustrated, irritated and cruel. Miriam is accepting, submissive, dumb. In addition Paul still belongs heart and soul to his mother. They decide to remain simply as friends and not to think of themselves as lovers.

Then Paul goes again to Willey Farm to meet Clara, who is visiting Miriam. Paul is obviously excited by Clara although he says that he does not like her. The three go for a walk together and Lawrence describes the tensions between them.

Next Paul goes to Lincoln with his mother. It is a perfect day and they are very happy together. Then we see Mrs Morel discussing the matter of Leonard's marriage to Annie (Paul's sister). Leonard, like Paul, has become sexually frustrated and insists on marrying Annie against cautious advice. When they have married and gone Mrs Morel and Paul discuss the business of sons and daughters leaving their mothers. Then it is Arthur's turn. He leaves the army and starts a relationship with Beatrice. In a brief scene we see these two together and feel the undercurrent of their sexual passion quite strongly.

For the remaining few pages we are back again with Paul; typically, we see him playing a physical game with Clara and writing a letter to Miriam. The chapter ends with yet another reference to his sexual frustration.

NOTES:

1. Easter. The major 'feast' of the Christian year, celebrating Christ's resurrection after the crucifixion.

2. Mary Queen of Scots. (see note 16 to Chapter 7, above)

3. Primitive Methodist Chapel. Chapel of this somewhat puritanical protestant sect.

4. Tartarin de Tarascon. A story by Alphonse Daudet, the French writer (published 1872).

5. Agnosticism. A view of the world which has increased in popularity in Europe since the end of the nineteenth century. An agnostic is someone who states that he does not know what the truth is about God or about the ultimate reality of the universe; the term can also be extended to include those who believe that it is in principle impossible to know about these things.

6. At the Renan 'Vie de Jésus' stage. One of the ways in which agnostics can continue to be close to Christianity is by considering Christ as an important teacher and great man, rather than as the Son of God. Ernest Renan's biography of Christ (*Vie de Jésus* is the French for *Life of Jesus*) was one of the first books to treat Christ entirely as a man (published 1863).

7. St John. That is, the Gospel according to St John in the Bible.

8. Can't stand 'Nevermore'. Paul is referring to a poem called 'The Raven' by Edgar Allan Poe (1804–1849). The raven (a black bird) visits the poet at night and puts his beak into the poet's heart. This symbolises the sorrow of the poet over his lost love. When he asks the raven to remove his beak and to leave, the bird answers 'Nevermore' ('Quoth the raven 'Nevermore'—'Quoth = 'said'.)

9. Deirdre or Iseult. Heroines of romantic legend, Gaelic and Arthurian respectively. Deirdre was intended by King Conor of Ulster to be his queen, but she ran away with Naoibe. He and his brother were treacherously murdered by Conor, who forced Deirdre to live with him. She committed suicide by wrecking a chariot. Iseult, La Beale, is the sister or daughter of the King of Ireland; Iseult, La Blanche Mains, also in Arthurian legend is the daughter of the Duke of Brittany and the wife of Tristram.

10. W.S.P.U. emblazoned on my shield. That is: 'with the letters W.S.P.U. written on my shield'. The letters mean 'Women's Social and Political Union', a feminist group.

11. Lincoln. An ancient cathedral city in the east of England.

12. Glory Hole ... Stone Bow ... Jew's House. Objects of interest to the visitor to Lincoln.

13. She could run like an Amazon. In Greek mythology the Amazons were a tribe of women who could undertake all the physical activities of men: fighting, riding, running.

14. Omar Khayyam. This Persian poet became famous in Britain through the free translation of his work by Edward Fitzgerald which was published in 1859.

GLOSSARY:

beas'es 'as:	beasts (animals) have
bent:	(*here*) type of grass
boon-companion:	constant friend
brazen imp:	a friendly way of saying 'cheeky' or 'impudent'
bull-terrier:	large breed of dog
clack:	noise of gate
cocks:	(*here*) piles of hay
couchant:	lying down (*a heraldic term*)
cowslips:	a type of wild flower
cracked:	(*here*) mad
damned cheek:	rudeness
dot:	(*here*) hit
dotty:	mad
druv:	drove
fag:	cigarette
furlough:	home leave
game-cock:	cock originally used for fighting
grouse:	(*here*) complain
hanky-pankyin':	playing
harping on:	continuing to think and talk about
hawthorn:	a tree or bush (*Crataegus oxyacantha*)
honeysuckle:	a plant (*Lonicera periclymenum*)
horse-rake:	horse-drawn agricultural implement
ikey:	proud
I've non got it:	I haven't got it
jowl:	(*here*) hit
knivey:	naughty
Ma:	mother
magenta:	bright purple colour
nag:	(*here*) keep reminding about something
nasturtiums:	a flower (*Tropaeolum majus*)
not a fat lot:	not much
pokey:	(*here*) small and dark

pore fing:	childish way of saying 'poor thing'
roadstead:	part of the sea where ships anchor
run the rig:	go through the whole process
scotch:	(*here*) interruption; prevention
staid body:	quiet and homely person
sup:	(*here*) drink
teem:	(*here*) pour out
thirty-four quid:	thirty-four pounds (£34)
tonic solfa:	simple music
toppling:	falling over
tussocky:	covered in small mounds or lumps
whiff:	a 'puff'; a mouthful of smoke
winder:	(*here*) a bad thing

Chapter 10: Clara

Paul wins another prize with a painting and sells it for twenty guineas. His mother is delighted. In the early pages of the chapter we see Paul and Mrs Morel discussing his success, the matter of class and the problem of his relations with women. He is drifting away from Miriam. He goes to visit Clara, who is living with her mother in a small house in Nottingham. This mother claims a lot of his attention; just as Mrs Leivers did.

Clara, living apart from her husband, is poor, and Paul arranges that she should come back to work at Jordan's, as she used to do before being married. Thus they see each other every day and a lot of this chapter is taken up with their conversations in the factory. She is not popular with the other girls working there because she is superior and because they adore Paul, who is only interested in Clara. Fanny, a hunchbacked girl, gives Paul some paints for his twenty-first birthday in a gesture of warm friendliness on the part of all the girls at the factory except 'the Queen of Sheba', Clara.

But Paul can see Clara outside working hours. In their lunch-break, one day, they walk together up to the castle and come quite close together. After that they repeat the walk often and Clara talks about the failure of her marriage. Paul feels that it may be her fault: perhaps she was not able to give herself to Baxter. The chapter ends with the positions reversed; Clara is questioning Paul about Miriam and we come to learn a lot about that relationship from his answers.

NOTES:

1. Twenty guineas. A guinea is one pound (£1) and one shilling (1s.). Shillings, which no longer exist, were worth 5 per cent of a pound, so a guinea is worth £1.05p in modern British coinage.

2. Socialist, Suffragette, Unitarian people. In other words 'advanced' or 'progressive' people. Suffragettes were women who demand the right to vote. Unitarians are relatively free-thinking Christians.

3. But she might as well be hung for a sheep as for a lamb. A proverbial expression meaning: when she had done a small wrong or stupid thing she would lose nothing by making it bigger.

4. That was a little, darkish room too. In this paragraph, and throughout the episode in Mrs Radford's house, Lawrence uses words connected with lace-making (web, clump, etc.). It is not necessary to understand all of these exactly; the general impression is that Mrs Radford's room is a small factory in which she and Clara are busy.

5. She's for ever on that 'igh horse of hers... 'To be on one's high horse' means to be proud and perhaps angry. The whole sentence means: 'She is so proud that one day her pride will be her undoing'.

6. Juno. In Classical mythology Juno is the queen of Jupiter, chief among the gods.

7. Lettres de mon Moulin. 'Letters from my mill.' A popular work by the French novelist Alphonse Daudet (1840–97).

8. Penelope. In Homer's *Odyssey* Penelope is the wife of the hero, Odysseus, who is thought to be dead; Penelope, as Queen of his island (Ithaca) is surrounded by lovers and suitors. She says she will choose from among the wooers when her weaving is finished; but she remains faithful, and goes on with her weaving, secretly unpicking it every night for many years until Odysseus returns.

9. The Queen of Sheba. Here means any grand, proud woman. See the Bible, First Book of Kings, 9.

GLOSSARY:

all on thorns:	excited and anxious
beguy:	way of saying 'By God'
blacklead:	(written in) pencil
blurted:	spoken suddenly and without thinking
bobbins:	part of lace-making equipment
buckled:	(*here*) got down to; undertook
doubted:	(*here*) feared
dowdy:	badly dressed
duck:	(*here*) dear
grit:	(*here*) courage
hieroglyph:	Egyptian writing composed of pictures
ikey:	proud
jennying:	spinning (making lace)

Jove!:	an exclamation of surprise
lavender:	(*here*) colour; pale mauve
lousy:	(*here*) bad; poor quality
mantled:	(*here*) came up
misdoubt:	doubt
piqued:	angered
plump:	(*here*) direct
rotten swank:	Paul uses this to show how he hates Clara's 'swank' or excessive pride
sang-froid:	(*French*) calm
shapen:	shaped
snap:	(*here*) argue with
somnambule:	sleep-walker
sweated:	this is an abbreviation for 'sweated labour', i.e. 'hard work'
tear:	(*here*) rage
terrific great shakes:	very important
toffies:	toffees
vast web of lace:	(see note 4 to this chapter, above)

Chapter 11: The test on Miriam

The 'test' in this important chapter is Paul's attempt to create a full relationship with Miriam. He seems to know that it is impossible and that something is wrong between them physically, and he is right. Although they do become lovers, it is not a success. The earlier part of the chapter is a long and intense build-up to Paul and Miriam's mutual loss of virginity; it reveals Lawrence's delicacy and accuracy in portraying human relationships. There is a peaceful episode when Miriam is staying alone in her grandmother's cottage and Paul visits her there. For one day he loves her 'utterly', but he realises that they will never be fulfilled with one another.

He decides to 'break off' with Miriam and announces this to his mother, who is sympathetic. He is more interested in Clara. The scene of the 'breaking off' is painful and Paul reacts by going into a public house where he flirts with some girls. He returns, really upset, to his mother.

NOTES:

1. **A Botticelli Madonna.** A picture of the Virgin Mary, Christ's mother, by Sandro Botticelli, the Italian master (1445–1510).

2. **Sir Thomas More.** One of the great humanists of the Renaissance in England, a politician, writer and Catholic martyr. He lived from 1478 to 1535. His *Utopia* is the most famous of his writings.

3. Not in the Gretchen way. That is, Miriam is unlikely to become pregnant. The reference, a rather coy one, is to Goethe's *Faust*, Part One.

4. The great Being. A way of referring to God.

5. Chemistry demonstrator. A junior lecturer at the university.

6. In the Moon and Stars. In a 'pub' or drinking-house. British 'pubs' have a variety of strange names.

7. The Willow Tree. Another 'pub'.

GLOSSARY:

blotch:	mark, vaguely outlined patch
clenched against:	(*here*) resistant to
crotchety:	eccentric; bad-tempered
iris:	a flower (*Iridacea*)
lark:	(*here*) game
Madonna lilies:	flowers (*Lilium candidum*)
nullity:	nothingness
pink:	(*here*) a flower (*Dianthus*)

Chapter 12: Passion

The test on Miriam having failed, Paul turns to Clara. He becomes increasingly obsessed by her and at last, in a long episode, they make love in the open air. Naturally he discusses her with his mother and, even, with Miriam. He then takes Clara to visit his home on a day when Miriam is also planning to visit the Morels. The tensions between Mrs Morel, Paul and the two girls are described. Paul takes Clara back to catch her train; she refuses to make love on the way to the station and we sense that something is wrong.

Next Paul and Clara go to the theatre together. In an astonishingly strong passage Lawrence describes the fever of desire which attacks Paul at this point and the wild frustration he feels when he and Clara return to her mother's house and the older woman's presence inhibits love-making. Typically, Mrs Radford, the mother, has a part to play in this scene, and it ends at breakfast when Paul asks Clara *and* Mrs Radford to go to the seaside with him for a couple of days.

NOTES:

1. Liberty's. (See Chapter 8, note 7).

2. Michael Angelo. (See Chapter 8, note 4).

3. The Isle of Wight. An island off the south coast of England, further away and more expensive than the other holiday-resorts mentioned in the novel.

4. The Queen of Sheba. What Clara is called by the girls at Jordan's. Means any grand, proud woman. (See the Bible, First Book of Kings, 9).

5. The Trent. This is the river that runs through Nottingham.

6. Little Kirke White. A Nottingham poet (1785-1806).

7. Britannia. The female personification of Britain, formerly featured on British coins.

8. And she bobbed a little curtsey. That is, she made the bowing and half-kneeling movement of respect used by women instead of a handshake until about the First World War.

9. I believe Eve enjoyed it . . . When Adam and Eve have broken God's commandment they are expelled from Eden (= earthly Paradise). (See the Bible, the Book of.Genesis, 3.)

10. Suffragette. Woman demanding the right to vote.

11. So she's already singled out from the sheep. Traditionally the separation of sheep (= goodness) from goats (= evil) is symbolic of God's judgement on the world.

12. Baptism. Lawrence uses this word metaphorically. Literally baptism is the ceremony which establishes a baby as a member of the Christian Church.

13. When I was a boy, I always thought a pillar of cloud by day . . . This is Paul's childhood explanation of the passage in the Bible where the Israelites are guided by cloud and fire through the desert. (See the Book of Exodus, 13.)

14. The bloodhound quality. Bloodhounds are dogs used, for example, by the police, because they are very good at following the scents left by people and animals.

15. Sarah Bernhardt. Famous French actress (1844-1923).

16. 'La Dame aux Camélias': A novel, written in 1848 by the younger Alexandre Dumas, a French writer, and dramatised by him in 1852.

17. Doomsday. The last day of the world; judgement day.

GLOSSARY:

annealed:	burnt in; fused together by fire
bad 'uns:	bad ones
barkled:	dirty
boxes your ears:	hits you on the head
bust:	(*here*) spend freely

chiffon:	a thin material
chrysanthemums:	flowers (*Chrysanthemum*)
crib, cribbage:	card game
crozzly:	crisp
dahlias:	flowers, named after Dr Dahl, a Swedish botanist
dash:	(*here*) polite way of saying 'Damn.'
dibbling:	playing lightly
Dutch oven:	oven near the fire in which things are kept warm
femme incomprise:	(*French*) misunderstood woman
grizzled:	with grey in his black hair
guyney:	here means something like 'chicken' or 'lad' or 'love'. Familiar expression of endearment
hollyhock spire:	tall part of a type of flower (*Althaea rosea*)
jaw:	(*here*) talk
jay:	a bird
kite:	toy which flies in the wind
lilacs:	shrubs (*Syringa vulgaris*)
mater:	(*Latin*) mother
Michaelmas daisies:	large flowers that bloom around Michaelmas (September 29th) (*Aster tripolium*)
my sirs!:	expression of surprise
osiers:	willow-trees
pierrot:	figure of a fancy-dress ball (See glossary to Chapter 3, above)
prop:	(*here*) stick
quid:	£1
ruffled:	untidy; disorganised
sang-froid:	(*French*) calmness
she'd as leave . . .:	she would prefer . . .
sixpenny hop:	dance
slag:	dirt cast up by the coal mine
smitten:	hit
sphinx:	legendary monster with an impassive woman's face
swanky:	boastful
tack:	(*here*) food
tinge:	(*here*) small amount
too-in:	bother; fuss
towzled:	ruffled; untidy
twitchel:	lane
twistin':	(*here*) worrying
vermilion:	bright red colour
waxy:	(*here*) angry
whittling:	(*here*) whining
worrit:	worry

Chapter 13: Baxter Dawes

Paul meets Baxter Dawes in a public house and they argue; Paul throws beer in Dawes's face and Dawes swears he will revenge himself. A bond of some sort seems to be growing up between Paul and the older man, but it is partly a bond of hatred and Clara is in the middle of it. There is an argument between the two men at Jordan's and Dawes is told to leave the factory by Mr Jordan.

We now see Clara and Paul together and Lawrence discusses their passionate relationship in some detail. One evening Paul meets Baxter at a lonely spot and they fight; Paul is quite badly hurt and becomes ill. When he recovers he feels that he no longer cares for Clara or for Miriam. He goes away for a few days' holiday with a man friend. When he returns he discovers that his mother is ill in Annie's house in Sheffield. He gets medical attention for her, makes his father visit her, and organises the family generally. She is brought back to Bestwood in a car, obviously dying.

NOTES:

1. **The Punch Bowl.** A public-house; drinking establishment.

2. **The man in righteousness arrayed.** Paul quotes one of the hymns he has learnt in 'chapel'.

3. **An imaginary Orpen.** Refers to the painter Sir William Orpen (1878–1931).

4. **The George or the White Horse.** Names of more 'pubs'.

5. **At Whitsuntide he said he would go to Blackpool.** Whitsun is a feast in the Christian calendar, celebrated in the early summer. Blackpool is a large seaside resort on the west coast of England, popular with the working classes for holidays.

6. **Sheffield.** Large industrial town a little to the north of Nottingham.

7. **That miserable Central.** The Central railway company (see note 3 to Chapter 4, above).

8. **Only a bit of a tumour.** In fact Mrs Morel has cancer.

9. **Ten guineas.** (See note 1 to Chapter 10, above). Ten guineas = £10.50p. (a lot of money for a miner before the First World War). In fact the doctor only charges eight guineas (= £8.40p.)

GLOSSARY:

begod: by God
behint-hand: (behind-hand) late

bob-tailed evening suit: evening suits, in the period referred to, had long 'tails' on the jackets. Paul's suit was without these

braggin': (bragging) showing-off; boasting

chagrin: (*French*) anger

cherchez-la-femme: (*French*) look for the woman

chucker-out: large man employed to throw trouble-makers out of public houses

cocksureness: extreme self-confidence

cow-parsnip: a large weed (*Heracleum Sphondylium*)

daggeroso: (*Italian*) someone carrying a knife

dunno: don't know

forget-me-not: a small blue flower (*Myosotis palustris*)

funk: be a coward; be afraid of

God blimey: God blind me (*swear-word*)

jiggered: exclamation of surprise

landed: (*here*) arrived

lardy-da: pejorative way of referring to somebody's upper-class qualities or snobbery

let on: (*here*) talked about

Lily of the valley: a flower (*Convallaria majalis*)

navvy: road-mender; labourer

nowt wi' a bleeder like you!: nothing with you! ('Bleeder' is a rude way of referring to someone)

rowdying: making noise and trouble

serve him jolly well right: he deserves that

shady: (*here*) evil-looking; dark

shay sho: say so

sod: (*here*) rude way of referring to someone

spit it out: (*here*) say it

strike me!: (*here*) expression of surprise

sweal: to burn or melt away

tart an' all: with a girlfriend too ('tart' is a rude way of referring to a girl)

tha art: (thou art) you are

tipping Mr Jenkinson the wink: giving Mr Jenkinson a private indication to act

to a 'T': exactly

trapse: long walk; great effort

whipperty-snappin': a strange expression meaning 'behaving like a whipper-snapper'. A 'whipper-snapper' is a boy or young man and the word is used in contempt

whoam: home

Chapter 14: The release

Paul visits Baxter Dawes in the hospital in Sheffield. Baxter has been ill and is out of work. Paul works at establishing a friendship with him and starts to bring Clara back to him.

Mrs Morel takes a long time to die and drives Paul and Annie nearly mad with anxiety and grief. Paul sees Baxter again and talks to Clara about his sorrow. Mrs Morel takes morphia to ease her pain and Paul at last decides to give her too much of this drug one night. The result is that, after hours of torment for her children while she remains just alive, she dies, killed, ironically, by her son. Paul's father is frightened and shrinks from a full realisation of his wife's death.

Paul is badly shaken and seems to be going into a despairing frame of mind. He goes to the seaside and invites Dawes to visit him there, then he invites Clara and leaves the husband and wife together to be reconciled.

NOTES:

1. **Jim Crow.** An American slang name for a metal implement. Here it is used because Baxter only says 'Caw' which is the noise supposedly made by the birds called crows.

2. **Colonel Seely's Home.** A convalescent home; that is, an institution for people recovering from illnesses or operations.

3. **The Other Land.** Heaven.

4. **Benger's.** A patent drink, based on hot milk, sometimes given to those who are ill.

GLOSSARY:

a bit down:	depressed
begod:	by God
caw!:	noise made by a crow
calceolarias:	flowers (*Scrophulariacea*)
chrysanthemums:	flowers (*Chrysanthemum*)
dahlias:	flowers named after Dr Dahl, a Swedish botanist
dunno:	don't know
Gad:	God
geraniums:	flowers (*Geraniacea*)
godsend:	lucky arrival; present from God
half-crown:	obsolete coin worth 12.5p.
Little:	(*here*) Paul's nick-name for his mother
nuit-blanche:	(*French*) night without sleep
owt:	any
pigeon:	(*here*) another of Paul's names for his mother

Sister:	(*here*) nurse
sithee:	look
sulk:	to be bad tempered like a child
waft:	to be blown about in the wind

Chapter 15: Derelict

As the title of this chapter implies, Paul is brought low at the end of the novel. Everything seems meaningless to him after his mother's death. Clara goes to Sheffield with Baxter, Morel goes to live with friends in Bestwood; there is no home left for Paul, no centre to his life. He moves into lodgings in Nottingham and suffers.

One day he meets Miriam and they go to his lodgings where they finally decide that they cannot marry one another or really continue as lovers at all. Paul repeats his intention of going abroad and takes Miriam home for the last time. The novel ends with Paul's bitter but not hopeless view of the universe, his repetition of the word 'mother' and his final decision to choose the lights of the town in preference to the darkness of death.

NOTES:
1. **The Unitarian Church.** Church of a small Protestant sect with some similarities to the Methodist and Congregationalist sects. (See note 2 to Chapter 10 above.)

GLOSSARY:

anemones:	flowers (*Anemone nemorosa*)
freesias:	flowers named after Dr Fries, a Swedish botanist
fume:	(*here*) smoke
mater:	(*Latin*) mother
snowdrops:	small flowers, usually the first to appear in the year in Britain (*Galanthus nivelis*)
tilting:	(*here*) running
weasel:	small, furry animal

Part 3

Commentary

The author's own view of the book

On 14 November 1912 Lawrence wrote a letter to his friend and patron Edward Garnett. In it he described *Sons and Lovers* as follows:

A woman of character and refinement goes into the lower class, and has no satisfaction in her own life. She has had a passion for her husband, so the children are born of passion, and have heaps of vitality. But as her sons grow up, she selects them as lovers—first the eldest, then the second. These sons are *urged* into life by their reciprocal love of their mother—urged on and on. But when they come to manhood, they can't love, because their mother is the strongest power in their lives, and holds them . . . As soon as the young men come into contact with women there is a split. William gives his sex to a fribble* and his mother holds his soul. But the split kills him, because he doesn't know where he is. The next son gets a woman who fights for his soul—fights his mother. The son loves the mother—all the sons hate and are jealous of the father. The battle goes on between the mother and the girl, with the son as object. The mother gradually proves the stronger, because of the tie of blood. The son decides to leave his soul in his mother's hands, and, like his elder brother, go for passion. Then the split begins to tell again. But, almost unconsciously, the mother realises what is the matter and begins to die. The son casts off his mistress, attends to his mother dying. He is left in the end naked of everything, with the drift towards death.

In this summary of the novel Lawrence draws attention to the mother-son theme. Miriam and Clara, in this account, are reduced almost to the level of symbolic characters with only a secondary function in the main mother-son relationship. Further, it is a Paul-centred view of the novel only after being a Mrs Morel-centred view.

This can be taken as evidence that Lawrence saw his novel as a study of the Oedipus complex. This psychological term was being employed by Sigmund Freud, the father of modern psychology, at about the same time as *Sons and Lovers* was being written. It refers to Freud's theory that all children are more or less affected by sexually-based feelings

*'fribble' means a trifler, an affected, trivial, weak, small-minded person, in this case William's Miss Western.

about their parents: particularly, boys will always have some form of desire for the mother and jealousy of the father. Clearly in *Sons and Lovers* Paul is very close indeed to an incestuous relationship with his mother. This is discussed further in section 6(a) below.

Sons and Lovers as autobiography

In the introduction, above, an account is given of Lawrence's life and some connections are made between his life and his novel. This relationship between his life and work is something we cannot escape from when dealing with Lawrence, and here it will be considered further. However, the novel is a picture of wider things than just Paul's soul: it is a picture of life in a Nottinghamshire mining community at the 'turn of the century' (that is, around 1900) and it is a picture of the intellectual spirit of those times. Thus we can see it (*i*) as a psychological novel (that is its centre, Paul Morel) with (*ii*) a 'ring' of sociology outside it (the Nottinghamshire mining community; the working-class environment of 1900) and then with (*iii*) a further 'ring', outside that, of intellectual history. We can look at these three facets of the novel in order.

(i) Paul Morel and D.H. Lawrence

Lawrence, later in life, insisted that the first part of *Sons and Lovers*, at least, was autobiography. The detailed, rich description of the Morel's home, and the passionate tone in which Lawrence talks about Paul and his feelings, warn us that we are reading something very close to the author's experience.

However, we also have objective evidence that the novel is about Lawrence's own childhood and adolescence in the 'Miriam Papers' first analysed by Harry T. Moore in his book *D.H. Lawrence: The Man and His Works* (1969). The 'Miriam Papers' are in fact documents which relate to the original of 'Miriam' (Jessie Chambers) and to her involvement with the writing of *Sons and Lovers*. The documents consist of some passages from the novel written in Jessie's own handwriting (they appear in the final work much expanded by Lawrence) and some comments by Jessie on Lawrence's own work. It is clear from these papers that, although Jessie often protests that Lawrence is changing the past in writing his novel, the basic plot, many incidents and many details, at least of the Miriam sections, are true to Jessie's memory. The fact that Lawrence was able to incorporate Jessie's own writings into the novel, in some cases without change, proves the point.

From a critical point of view the 'Miriam Papers' provide a warning. Jessie never realised that fiction is a different kind of writing from history or biography. In her comments on *Sons and Lovers* she seems to accept that the *facts* are 'true' but objects when Lawrence starts to embroider them. She applies the test of factuality to the novel and finds it does not pass, but no novel could or should pass that test.

(ii) Nottinghamshire in 'Sons and Lovers'

Lawrence's country, the Midlands, at the time of *Sons and Lovers*, was balanced between an old, rural world and a new, industrial world. The novel opens with a description in which the two worlds are strangely mixed. In the first paragraph are mentioned coal-pits, with the black places they make, and collier's houses in the same sentences as brooks (streams), cornfields, meadows and farms. Even when the new nine-teenth-century mines arrive at Bestwood (in the second paragraph) the first one is opened 'on the edge of Sherwood Forest'.

Morel is a typical product of the Industrial Revolution (a period of British history which can be said to extend from 1750 to 1850 approximately but whose effects are still with us today). He is a cog in the machine of a large company, he lives in a small and rather ugly rented house and even, towards the end of the novel, goes on strike. But he walks across the fields to work. Paul is alive to nature in a remarkable way especially after he has started to visit Willey Farm. Perhaps Morel's mine and the Leivers' farm symbolise this division in the book between industrial and agricultural.

Nottingham is a large town with a certain amount of industry; Jordan's, although it is an unusual factory, is certainly a factory and it has many of the characteristics of the nineteenth-century industrial establishment: it is large and rather dark, the hours of work are long and the wages are not very good. On the other hand Paul and Clara can make love in the open, by the River Trent, only a short distance outside Nottingham. Then again, Nottingham was famous for its manufacture of lace (Mrs Radford and Clara make lace, it will be remembered) and in the novel is clearly thriving economically as a town. But Paul often walks to Bestwood across the fields, and in his lodgings in Nottingham at the end of the novel are flowers: anemones and freesias.

When Paul and Clara walk up to Nottingham Castle together in Chapter 10 they look down at the town and the country around it:

> Great stretches of country darkened with trees and faintly brightened with corn-land, spread towards the haze, where the hills rose blue beyond the grey.
> 'It is comforting', said Mrs Dawes, 'to think the town goes no farther. It is only a *little* sore upon the country yet.'
> 'A little scab,' Paul said.

Clearly here the country is seen as superior to the town and certainly we feel generally that Willey Farm and those who work there are in some way healthier, more 'natural' than the people at Jordan's or even in the mines. On the other hand, Paul says to Clara, a little later in the same conversation, 'But the town's all right . . . it's only temporary. This is the crude, clumsy make-shift we've practised on, till we found out what the idea is. The town will come all right.' So perhaps Lawrence is not so simple as just to say that the rural is good while the urban is bad. The point is that he was fascinated by nature and all through the novel describes landscape, flowers and animals very intensely, but he was also fascinated by the dark masses working in the factories and by the freshness of some aspects of working-class life. Nottinghamshire provided both sides of this double fascination.

(iii) The years 1900–1914 in 'Sons and Lovers'

This period is sometimes called the Edwardian period, after King Edward VII who reigned from the death of Queen Victoria in 1901 to his own death in 1910. The period is extended to the outbreak of the First World War in 1914. *Sons and Lovers* was published in 1913, of course, and its early chapters must correspond to a period back in the 1880s, but its main time-focus is on the years of Paul's adolescence and early manhood (1900–1910 if we accept Paul as a portrait of Lawrence). The novel was written during the years 1910–1913. It is a marvellous portrait of the 'other side' of Edwardian England. It is not concerned with the upper-class life of the times which is what Englishmen normally think of when the word 'Edwardian' is used. It is limited to a small unexciting part of the provinces and it deals largely with working-class folk. Because of this limitation it gives us a remarkably detailed picture of one small aspect of the life of the period.

In some ways, however, the novel fails to be a portrait of the age. A good example of this is to be found in Paul's painting. In the great world of London and Paris the main streams of modern art were starting to flow vigorously during the decade 1900–1910. Cézanne, Gauguin, Pissarro and others reached the height of their fame at this time and died, leaving a generation of positively twentieth-century painters such as Picasso, Matisse and Braque who were beginning to astonish the world. But not a breath of this comes into *Sons and Lovers*. Paul is very much a provincial boy making his way with some unadventurous paintings which the Nottinghamshire gentry will buy.

On the other hand, an age or period is not only made by great men in great cities; in *Sons and Lovers* we can feel some of the forces at work during the period as they affect the humble and obscure. Thus, for instance, Miriam is an isolated, unrealistic, romantic woman, not very careful about work but passionately careful about her religion: she is the product of generations of under-educated and under-employed women. Clara is a small version of the new, independent 'Suffragette', the woman who can leave her husband and join the Women's Social and Political Union. Lawrence enables us to understand quite well how difficult life was for such women and he sets Clara's political ideals against all sorts of realistic foils: her poverty, her pity for Baxter, her passion for Paul as a man, and so on.

Sons and Lovers is not really a social history, however, and its main interests is in spiritual and psychological developments which can only be fully understood when we have discussed Lawrence's philosophy (see pages 62–3 of these notes).

The structure of *Sons and Lovers*

The novel has an unusual and rather 'modern' structure. A summary of its plot seems simple enough: the novel covers the period from the Morels' courtship and marriage to the time when Paul is about twenty-five years old, roughly the period from 1880 to 1910. In general this summary is accurate, the first chapters cover the Morels' marriage and later chapters deal with Paul's birth, his growing up, his love affairs and so on, but within this general scheme Lawrence moves about very freely indeed and treats time-developments as being of less importance than psychological or spiritual developments.

Chapter 4 ('The Young Life of Paul') provides an example. It opens with a general description of Paul as a boy that applies to him at any age between five and fifteen. Typically Lawrence says things like 'As a rule he seemed old for his years', and 'As he grew older he became stronger'. These general statements develop into a specific story without our noticing it: Paul's sister Annie 'adored him'; she had a big doll: she put the doll on the sofa; 'meantime Paul must practise jumping off the sofa arm'; he does jump and he breaks the doll and we find that we are in the middle of a specific incident which is presented to us vividly: Paul and Annie burn the doll as a sacrifice. When this is over Lawrence is back at the general level again: 'All the children, but particularly Paul, were peculiarly *against* their father, along with their mother . . .' but immediately he starts to narrate another specific incident: 'Paul never forgot coming home from the Band of Hope one Monday evening . . .' and we hear about William's fight with his father.

Another example can be found in Chapter 10, 'Clara'. This chapter opens with the words 'When he was twenty-three years old . . .' and at first Lawrence moves steadily forward from this point making general observations such as 'Paul and his mother now had long discussions about life' or specific references to time such as 'The months went slowly along.' Within this forward movement there are general descriptions of this whole period of Paul's life and specific details are narrated from it. Then, rather surprisingly, we find a paragraph starting 'When he celebrated his twenty-third birthday, the house was in trouble.' We are then given a description of an incident that took place on Paul's birthday; this enables Lawrence to move into several pages in which he narrates Paul's first walk out of Jordan's with Clara, also on his birthday. Then we find we are back at the general level and are being told about this whole phase of Paul's relationship with Clara: 'They walked out together very often at dinner-time'.

In these examples, and in most of the other chapters, Lawrence selects the details, incidents and episodes which he wants and puts them into his general movement forwards (the movement of Paul's development) wherever it suits him to do so. He is not at all a slave to a simple time-sequence.

As a smaller example than the examples given above, we can look at the incident of Mrs Morel's hat, towards the end of Chapter 4. Mrs Morel is at the market trying to decide whether to buy a certain small dish. Lawrence describes her as 'a little woman, in a bonnet and a black costume'. Then he picks up this detail of her bonnet (hat) and inserts these short paragraphs:

> Her bonnet was in its third year; it was a great grievance to Annie.
> 'Mother!' the girl implored, 'don't wear that nubbly little bonnet.'
> 'Then what else shall I wear?' replied the mother tartly. 'And I'm sure it's right enough.'
> It has started with a tip; then had had flowers; now was reduced to black lace and a bit of jet.
> 'It looks rather come down', said Paul. 'Couldn't you give it a pick-me-up?'
> 'I'll jowl your head for impudence', said Mrs Morel, and she tied the strings of the black bonnet valiantly under her chin.

That is the entire incident; the next sentence is 'She glanced at the dish again'. There is no indication as to whether the exchange about the bonnet takes place before, after or at the same time as the shopping episode in which Mrs Morel is buying the little dish. The mention of the word 'bonnet' reminds Lawrence of Mrs Morel's rather pathetic attachment to her poor hat and he breaks off the story about the dish to tell us about this.

The point is that the exact time-sequence is not important. What is important is that we should get the strongest and most accurate impression of Mrs Morel and her relationship with her children. This is a novel of psychological and emotional truth rather than detailed surface realism.

Another aspect of the structure of *Sons and Lovers* concerns Lawrence's use of a varying point of view. Often the action is described directly by the author-narrator, but at times it is presented through the eyes of Paul, or of his mother or even of Miriam. Almost never do we see things through the eyes of Clara or Morel or the other characters.

This question of authorial point of view is complex and difficult but it is worth asking—about any part of the novel—the question 'Through whose eyes are we seeing this?'. For example, do we not see both Miriam and Clara through Paul's eyes, at least at times? Of course, a lot of the novel is written in dialogue, which means that we are often given the exact words and point of view of the speaker; however, those parts of the novel which are not dialogue offer us points of view that vary rapidly and subtly. Let us look at this example from Chapter 10; it describes Paul:

> He went out to dinner in his evening suit that had been William's. Each time his mother's heart was firm with pride and joy. He was started now.

Here the first two sentences come from the mind of the narrator but the third sentence, although it is also written in the third person, clearly comes from Mrs Morel's mind. *She* is thinking to herself 'Now he's started' and we see Paul from *her* point of view. The next sentence is again set back in the mind of the narrator, so we have four words in the middle of a paragraph which offer a brief change of the novel's point of view. Such variations are easy to miss. Here is another, very similar, example:

> Paul was wild with joy for his mother's sake. She would have a real holiday now. (Chapter 7)

The first of these sentences is an objective description of Paul's emotion while the second of them offers us Paul's point of view on this emotion.

The style of *Sons and Lovers*

Lawrence's style is the natural result of his intentions in the novel. He is not telling an exciting story with a gripping plot, he is presenting a 'portrait of the artist', a psychological study of growth. His style is therefore one of explanation, direct statement and the expression of his own views about Paul Morel, his family and his life. On the other hand, he is also trying to express his sense of the importance and even sacredness of nature, of the human body and of human relationships, so there is another element in his style: besides being direct and explanatory it is also at times poetic, rich and resonant. In addition to these 'two styles' there are some special features of the prose of *Sons and Lovers* that must be considered, notably Lawrence's use of dialect.

Lawrence's direct, explanatory style

In his later novels Lawrence sometimes became more of a lecturer than a novelist and he has been criticised for his rather crude preaching in such novels as *Kangaroo* (1923) and *The Plumed Serpent* (1926). In *Sons and Lovers* this tendency to preach is present, but it is well under control. It is Lawrence, for example, who tells us of Morel, the father, that 'he had denied the God in him'. The statement does not emerge from the novel as a possibility to be discussed, it is simply handed to us as a truth.

This may worry us if we prefer our novels not to be sermons, but for the most part Lawrence's frankness in *Sons and Lovers* is a good rather than a bad thing. As an example we can consider this paragraph from Chapter 11 in which we are presented with Paul's feeling that his love-making with Miriam is an inevitable failure:

> He continued faithful to Miriam. For one day he had loved her utterly. But it never came again. The sense of failure grew strong. At first it was only a sadness. Then he began to feel he could not go on. He wanted to run, to go abroad, anything. Gradually he ceased to ask her to have him.

These short, blunt sentences express as directly as possible the movement of Paul's mind. Their tone is somehow solid and monotonous and they convey a sense of the inevitability of his failure with Miriam and of his feelings of frustration and desperation. This example shows Lawrence at his most direct, we know exactly *what* he is telling us. Often, too, his directness has an explanatory purpose and we find ourselves being told clearly *why* certain things are so. For instance there is the following paragraph in Chapter 4:

> Paul loved to sleep with his mother. Sleep is still most perfect, in spite of hygienists, when it is shared with a beloved. The warmth, the security and peace of soul, the utter comfort from the touch of the other, knits the sleep, so that it takes the body and soul completely in its healing. Paul lay against her and slept, and got better . . .

Here Lawrence is quite unembarrassed by his explanation. The two sentences beginning 'Paul' could easily stand on their own but he adds the two sentences in between them as a general comment on sleep and the importance of physical touch. They are a lecturer's 'aside', a deliberate move from the particular subject under discussion (Paul) and the general implications of that subject ('the touch of the other').

A good deal of *Sons and Lovers* is taken up with conversation, and here again Lawrence has a direct approach which cuts out all unnecessary words and gives us the important part of any given dialogue. One of the reasons for this may be that in the Midland working-class environment of the novel people are not given to many words anyway; there is a kind of 'no-nonsense' approach to life which shortens the speech even of mother and son, as this example shows:

> One day he [Paul] came home at dinner-time feeling ill. But it was not a family to make any fuss.
> 'What's the matter with *you?*' his mother asked sharply.
> 'Nothing', he replied.
> But he ate no dinner.
> 'If you eat no dinner, you're not going to school,' she said.
> 'Why?' he asked.
> 'That's why.'

And with this answer ('That's why' here means that Mrs Morel refuses to offer any explanation) Paul goes to sleep on the sofa. The dialogue is brief, pointed, clear. No doubt mother and son exchanged more words on this occasion but Lawrence only gives us the words important for his purposes.

The conversation at the Morels', and among the miners, is brief and vivid. The conversation between Paul and Miriam or Paul and Clara is slightly more elaborate but, again, it is economically handled. Lawrence picks up a piece of dialogue just long enough for us to follow the argument that is going on and then drops it and goes back to description or analysis. This is another way in which he moves from the general (description, analysis) to the specific (part of one particular conversation) as described above. Here is an example. Clara is 'mad with desire' for Paul and he objects when she kisses him at work:

> 'But what do you always want to be kissing and embracing for?' he said. 'Surely there's a time for everything.'
> She looked up at him, and the hate came into her eyes.
> '*Do* I always want to be kissing you?' she said.
> 'Always, even if I come to ask you about the work. I don't want anything to do with love when I'm at work. Work's work . . .'
> 'And what is love?' she asked. 'Has it to have special hours?'
> 'Yes; out of work hours.'
> 'And you'll regulate it according to Mr Jordan's closing time?'
> 'Yes; and according to the freedom from business of any sort.'
> 'It is only to exist in spare time?'
> 'That's all, and not always then—not the kissing sort of love.'
> 'And that's all you think of it?'
> 'It's quite enough.'
> 'I'm glad you think so.'

The entire conversation is noted here as Lawrence gives it. Immediately before it he has been explaining how Clara becomes irritating to Paul with her insistence on constant passion. Immediately after it he explains the reaction of Paul to Clara's anger and then turns to their visit to the seaside. What he is aiming at in presenting this brief dialogue is not to 'advance the plot' or even to put much emphasis on *this* particular conversation: his aim is to give us yet another insight into the whole quality of the relationship. Thus he throws everything in, moving backwards and forwards in time, to reveal as much as possible about the relationship.

Lawrence's poetic style

Some aspects of existence, for Paul Morel and for Lawrence himself, have a religious, sacred quality which the novelist tries to catch by adopting a style that is more elevated, more 'poetic' and richer than his 'direct' style. This is particularly apparent when Lawrence is concerned with nature and with sex; the best examples of it are to be found at those points where Paul has an intense experience involving both of these things.

In Chapter 7 ('Lad-and-girl love') Paul and Miriam, still very much virgins, are walking together in the woods at nine o'clock at night. It is a magical occasion and Lawrence's style rises to meet it. 'There was a coolness in the wood, a scent of leaves, of honeysuckle, and a twilight. The two walked in silence. Night came wonderfully there, among the throng of dark tree-trunks.' Miriam wants to show Paul a rose bush she has discovered, 'She knew it was wonderful. And yet, till he had seen it, she felt it had not come into her soul. Only he could make it her own, immortal. She was dissatisfied.' Lawrence describes the dew, the mist, a 'cloud' of white flowers, Miriam's eagerness as she looks for her rose bush and the 'communion' she will be able to have with Paul once she finds it. They walk on into the wood until they find the bush:

> When they turned the corner of the path she stood still. In the wide walk between the pines, gazing rather frightened, she could distinguish nothing for some moments; the greying light robbed things of their colour. Then she saw her bush. . . .
>
> It was very still. The tree was tall and straggling. It had thrown its briers over a hawthorn-bush, and its long streamers trailed thick, right down to the grass, splashing the darkness everywhere with great spilt stars, pure white. In bosses of ivory and in large splashed stars the roses gleamed on the darkness of foliage and stems and grass. Paul and Miriam stood close together, silent, and watched. Point after point the steady roses shone out to them, seeming to kindle something in their souls. The dusk came like smoke around, and still did not put out the roses.

Paul and Miriam look into one another's eyes and have the 'communion' that she wants. The cool scent of the white roses, however, is 'a white, virgin scent' which makes Paul feel 'anxious and imprisoned'.

The vocabulary in all this tends to bring together the magic of nature and the magic of sexual attraction, although this is unrecognised. It is necessary for Paul to be present if Miriam is to experience her roses fully. There is a strong religious current in the episode and altogether Lawrence manages to make the physical (the roses; Paul's desire for Miriam) blend in with the spiritual (the 'communion'; the relationship between Paul and Miriam; their 'kindled' souls.) He does this by putting nature before us vividly and poetically, repeating key words (in the complete episode, which occupies about a page and a half, 'dark' or 'darkness' appear six times, 'white' five times, 'roses' five times, 'silent' or 'silence' four times, 'dusk', 'ivory', 'holy', 'honeysuckle', 'communion', 'stars', 'pines' and 'grass' twice each.) The magic atmosphere of the dusky wood with its scent-laden air is emphasised by these repetitions which take us a long way from the hard realities of, say, Morel's work down the mine.

The imagery used in the episode strengthens this impression. White flowers appear 'in a cloud', the sky is 'like mother-of-pearl', the roses 'splash' the darkness, 'gleam' in the darkness and 'shine', the dusk is 'like smoke', the roses seem like 'butterflies'. Everything becomes submerged in the half-light and everything seems to echo everything else: the mist is white as are the campion-flowers, and the sky, and the roses, and the ivory they remind us of, and certain sorts of butterfly, and Miriam's soul, and virginity, and the dresses of children at 'communion'. These are the techniques of poetry.

Lawrence adopts this 'poetic' style at several points in the novel and usually these are the significant moments, especially from a sexual point of view, in Paul's relationships. Thus there is an extensive description of the natural surroundings on the occasion of Paul and Clara's first love-making (Chapter 12) and Lawrence concludes the episode with this poetic image:

> When she arose, he, looking on the ground all the time, saw suddenly sprinkled on the black wet beech-roots many scarlet carnation petals, like splashed drops of blood; and red, small splashes fell from her bosom, streaming down her dress to her feet.

Perhaps Lawrence's style reaches its most elevated level in the next chapter (Chapter 13) when Paul is beginning to experience the impersonality of passion. He is simply man and Clara is simply woman and they become one with the natural world in which they make love. There is a section in the middle of this chapter which is devoted to a poetic treatment of this passionate communing with nature. It is also too long to quote in full but this, which is perhaps its climax, shows Lawrence at his most powerful:

> And after such an evening they both [Clara and Paul] were very still, having known the immensity of passion. They felt small, half afraid, childish, and wondering, like Adam and Eve when they lost their innocence and realised the magnificence of the power which drove them out of paradise and across the great night and the great day of humanity. It was for each of them an initiation and a satisfaction. To know their own nothingness, to know the tremendous living flood which carried them always, gave them rest within themselves. If so great a magnificent power could overwhelm them, identify them altogether itself, so that they knew they were only grains in the tremendous heave that lifted every grass-blade its little height, and every tree, and living thing, then why fret about themselves?

This dynamic prose takes us back to the first point made about Lawrence's style—it is like a piece of preaching, it is a lecture delivered in passionate tones and with the poetry of rhetoric.

Lawrence's use of dialect

Some of the Nottinghamshire dialect used in *Sons and Lovers* is explained in the notes to each chapter, above, especially in the notes to Chapter 1.

To some extent Lawrence's use of this Midland dialect is simply realism. Nottinghamshire miners do not speak the English of London or of the BBC and in 1913 the differences were even greater than they are today. However, there is more to it than just this. The dialect represents and symbolises certain changes and developments of character, class and mood.

Mrs Morel speaks better English than Morel who always speaks in dialect. She was once attracted by being 'Thee'd and thou'd' by Morel but for most of the novel the miner seems brutal while his wife is refined and part of the reason for this is the way in which they speak.

In the early chapters the children (William and Annie) speak in dialect but William, particularly, soon drops his accent as he moves up in the world and when he comes home from London (where he is becoming a gentleman) he only speaks normal English. His snobbish Miss Western speaks like a lady and we feel the contrast between her speech and Morel's when they are introduced.

The young Paul speaks in dialect but rapidly loses it so that there is a strong contrast, later in the novel, between him and Baxter Dawes, who always speaks dialect. Interestingly, he reverts to dialect after he has made love to Clara for the first time (Chapter 12). His first words

are 'Your flowers are smashed' (normal English), then he says 'Why
dost look so heavy?' (dialect: 'Why do you look so sad?') and 'Nay! . . .
Never thee bother!' (dialect: 'No! . . . You should not mind!') and 'But
tha shouldna worrit!' (dialect: 'But you should not worry!') and
'Dunna thee worrit' (dialect: 'Don't you worry'). But when he and
Clara have climbed back up to the top of the Grove he says 'Now we're
back at the ordinary level' (normal English). It seems here that the
'ordinary level' means not only the path at the top of the steep river-
bank but also the level of daily life which is 'ordinary' compared with
the level of love-making.

The dialect, then, seems suitable for the earthy but wonderful level of
passion (even Morel has the virtue of passionateness and he is earthy
too) but the 'ordinary level' requires normal English.

Miriam, significantly, always speaks normal English.

The characters in *Sons and Lovers*

This alphabetical list of the main characters in the novel gives a summary of their personalities and significance within the plot. The list uses
the name most frequently employed for the character by Lawrence,
thus Miriam, for example, comes under 'M' for Miriam rather than 'L'
for Leivers.

Annie Morel. The second of the Morel children. She appears in Chapter
1 as a girl of five 'whining' to go to the 'wakes'; then as a virtual
servant to Miss Western when Miss Western visits the Morels with
William; then as a trainee teacher; and then, rather more extensively,
during the period leading up to Mrs Morel's death (Chapters 13 and
14). Mrs Morel, in fact, is taken ill during her visit to Annie's house
in Sheffield; Annie has moved there after marrying Leonard. Altogether Annie is overshadowed by her brothers; not being a son she
cannot be her mother's 'lover'.

Arthur Morel. The least important and youngest of the sons. He is his
father's favourite (and least in competition for his mother's favour).
He is 'a spoilt and very good-looking boy'. He gets into trouble, and
into the army, but seems to have enough charm and character to get
out of trouble and to tolerate the army. Lawrence comments towards
the end that Arthur never was very closely bound into the family.

Beatrice Wyld. Appears in Chapter 8 and flirts with Paul in the presence
of Miriam. This shows up Miriam's seriousness and coldness in con-
trast with 'Beat' who is prepared to kiss and make jokes with Paul.
There is a similar scene in Chapter 9 where she is flirting with Arthur.
In spite of her joking it is apparent that she has a real passion for
Arthur who marries her as soon as he leaves the army.

Clara Dawes. First appears early in Chapter 8, heavy, blonde, defiant, and does not reappear until late in Chapter 9. We always see her through the powerful sexual effect she has on Paul. In Chapter 10 (which is called 'Clara') Paul visits Clara at her home in Nottingham where she lives with her mother, Mrs Radford. Then Clara starts to work again at Jordan's and she and Paul develop a rather difficult relationship there together. In Chapter 12 they make love and their relationship reaches its high point in their sexual fulfilment. Thereafter Clara starts to move back towards her husband, Baxter. She is the opposite of Miriam: she is large and physical and has advanced ideas where Miriam is small and spiritual with traditional and romantic views. Clara is body where Miriam is soul.

Baxter Dawes. Clara's husband. A rough working-class man who is in some ways the opposite of Paul: Baxter is heavy and vulgar against Paul's high intellectuality but they share a capacity for passion.

Edgar Leivers. One of Miriam's brothers at Willey Farm. Paul develops a special relationship with him after initial suspicion. Edgar represents nature in the sense that he is a countryman who helps Paul to learn about the farm.

Mr Jordan. Owner and manager at Jordan's. A typical nineteenth-century caricature. Jordan is not a bad man but he seems rather fussy and self-important. Lawrence's view of him has the quality of the working man's view of 'the boss'.

Mrs Leivers. Miriam's mother. In Chapter 6 she is shown in comparison with Paul's mother; where Mrs Morel can manage life and will fight with and for her men, Mrs Leivers seems to have given up and retreated into a spirituality which she has passed on to Miriam.

Leonard. Is a pleasant young man who marries Annie. He forms a comparison with Paul in his sexual desires which are portrayed in his discussion (Chapter 9) with Mrs Morel about his need to get married.

Miriam Leivers. First appears when Paul and Mrs Morel go up to Willey Farm (Chapter 6) aged fourteen. Then Lawrence opens Part Two of the novel with a description of her as a 'romantic heroine' and as a spiritual girl. But she develops physically into a girl both beautiful and womanly. She is shy, intense, devoted, religious, and she loves Paul increasingly. She is 'defeated' in her battle with Mrs Morel for Paul's soul (Chapter 9) and loses Paul to Clara, who is more physically fulfilling. But the last episode in the novel shows Paul with her and although they decide that they cannot marry it is significant that she is the last woman mentioned. As the guardian of his intellect she is more important than Clara, the guardian of his body. Miriam is always a secondary character, a reflection of Paul's dominance.

Mrs Morel. Is present in all the chapters of the novel except the last. She is short and quite strong physically. Paul calls her 'Little' (for 'Little Woman') and she resists childbirth and other problems without difficulty. Psychologically, too, she is strong, far stronger than Morel. He is hot, quick-tempered, passionate; she is firm and unyielding, expecting much from her men, and 'Cowd as death!' ('Cowd' = 'cold') as Morel says when she washes his back. Her movement upwards in the world, symbolised by her intellectual interests (she reads the newspaper and belongs to a discussion group), and by her pride in Paul's refinement, makes her typical of an emerging group of working-class women. Her strength as the centre of the Morel family occasionally seems as though, in a different world, it might be converted into a more public energy. Her death is in some ways the climax of the novel.

Morel. Lawrence felt later in his life that he had been unfair to this character who represents his father. Morel is pure working-class, a miner content to remain in the same position all his life, cheerful, quick-tempered, barely able to read and write. Independent in a foolish way (he always has arguments with his superiors in the mine) and careless (he is always having accidents) he is nonetheless a good workman and a popular character. Altogether he is a mixture of good and bad but our overall impression of him is one of weakness compared with his wife's strength.

Mr Pappleworth. A caricature of a senior clerk, Pappleworth is Paul's immediate superior at Jordan's (Chapter 5).

Paul Morel. The hero whose first quarter-century of life is the subject of the novel. He is a self-portrait by Lawrence and his body and soul are the focus of interest in the book.

Mrs Radford. Clara Dawes's mother, appears in Chapters 10 and 12 as a mother-figure who seems to stand between Paul and Clara rather as Mrs Morel stands between Paul and Miriam.

Lily Western. Miss Western is William Morel's London girl-friend. She is exaggeratedly mindless, trivial and vain. The point is that William cannot have a real relationship with a real woman because he 'belongs' to his mother; so he only gets this 'doll'.

William Morel. Is in some ways an early version of Paul. His death ends Part One of the novel and Part Two shows Paul going through, in much greater detail, some of the trials that William has already faced. William, like Paul and to some extent like his mother, starts to move up in the world. He represents the hard-working boy from the provinces who 'makes good' in London.

The main themes of *Sons and Lovers*

Love, sex and marriage

The novel opens with a picture of the Morels' marriage. Mrs Morel was attracted to Morel by 'the golden softness of this man's sensuous flame of life, that flowed off his flesh like the flame from a candle' (Chapter 1). She marries him and love, sex and marriage are brought together for a moment in a way they never are again in the novel. Problems arise because of other considerations, 'higher' than sensuality. Mrs Morel, a 'Puritan', tries to refine and elevate her husband; when she fails she starts to despise him and tries again, first with William and then with Paul.

This introduces into the novel the theme of the Oedipus complex. Paul, and William to some extent, love their mother in a way that certainly includes a sexual element. Paul often kisses his mother and talks to her as to a lover; at the end of Chapter 8, he tries to persuade his mother not to sleep in the same bed as his father. She refuses to sleep elsewhere than in her own room and when Paul escorts her upstairs he kisses her 'close' and goes to bed in a fury of what must be jealousy.

The main movement of the novel, from the point of view of love, however, concerns Paul's development away from the obsession with his mother towards a fulfilling relationship with other women. Miriam seems to offer love but she is unable to offer herself physically and Lawrence is at some pains to stress this difficulty. In Chapter 7, for example, he says that:

> All the life of Miriam's body was in her eyes, which were usually dark as a church . . . Her body was not flexible and living . . . There was no looseness or abandon about her. Everything was gripped stiff with intensity . . .

We feel Paul's frustration increasing as he continues his relationship with this soulful and awkward girl. All their activities together as 'Lad-and-girl' rest uncomfortably on Miriam's sexlessness. Even when Paul tries to teach her algebra, and becomes angry when she is slow at understanding, his anger has a sexual quality that implies the frustration of the relationship:

> He had been too fast. But he said nothing. He questioned her more, then got hot. It made his blood rouse to see her there, as it were, at his mercy, her mouth open, her eyes dilated with laughter that was afraid . . .

The word 'blood', in Lawrence's work, often has a sexual connotation. Although Miriam does eventually give herself to Paul physically the encounter is not successful and when they talk of getting married (and they even consider this as late as the last chapter of the novel) we immediately feel that it is an impossible idea.

Clara is Paul's next attempt at love. From the first moment that we see her Clara is presented as a physical being, in opposition to Miriam, and as extremely sexual. When Paul first sees her Lawrence has this to say:

> [Miriam was with] a rather striking woman, blonde, with a sullen expression, and a defiant carriage. It was strange how Miriam in her bowed, meditative bearing, looked dwarfed beside this woman with the handsome shoulders. Miriam watched Paul searchingly. His gaze was on the stranger, who ignored him. The girl saw his masculine spirit rear its head.

Later Paul tells Miriam that what he likes about Clara is that 'there's a sort of fierceness somewhere in her'. He says that if Miriam were to put red berries in her hair she would look like a 'witch or priestess' but could not look like a 'reveller', as Clara could. Clara is passion where Miriam is frigidity.

Inevitably Paul is attracted to this passion. He himself is intensely physical, as even Miriam recognises, and he becomes fascinated by Clara's heavy body, her 'sulky abandon'. Driven on by his feelings Paul first tries to develop a sexual relationship with Miriam (Chapter 11); this is not successful but in the attempt Paul does learn 'the great hunger and impersonality of passion', this frightens Miriam who wants Paul to be *hers*, but he cannot be because 'she took all and gave nothing . . . she gave no living warmth'. (As with his description of Morel, Lawrence uses the living and warm as positives against such negatives as death and coldness.) When, in Chapter 12, Paul turns to Clara for 'Passion' (which is the title of the chapter), their successful relationship comes as a sort of cure for his soul that has been wounded by unsatisfied desire.

Lawrence makes it clear that there is a positive value in this love-making with Clara. It is one of the major climaxes of the novel. True, Paul and Clara have to split up, perhaps because her heavy sensuality, like Miriam's frigidity, is limited and insufficient; but before they split up Lawrence devotes some of his best and strongest writing to their relationship. For Paul it is 'a sort of baptism of fire in passion', it is a satisfaction and a torture, the latter, for example, when Paul and Clara are at the theatre together and Lawrence depicts the tension of desire and frustration brilliantly. He even refers to the 'torture of nearness' which Paul suffers (Chapter 12). However, it is once again the 'impersonality' of passion that destroys the relationship: it makes them like 'Adam and Eve,' frightened by the power which overwhelms them, but then, afterwards:

> He had considerable peace, and was happy in himself. It seemed
> almost as if he had known the baptism of fire in passion, and it left
> him at rest. But it was not Clara. It was something that happened
> because of her, but it was not her. They were scarcely any nearer
> each other. It was as if they had been blind agents of a great force.
> (Chapter 13)

Besides the relationships of Paul we also see the sexuality of William
(although it is not clear quite how far his relationship with Miss Western
has gone in this direction), which is largely rendered negative by his
mother. Some clear hints are dropped about Leonard's desire for Annie
and about Arthur's passion for Beatrice. We have already seen that Mrs
Morel's passion for her husband is a basic question underlying the
novel.

This sexuality in the novel has been stressed because the whole purpose of the book, the tracing of Paul's development, almost seems to
get taken over by the development of his sex-life. Nonetheless the novel
concerns love. In Lawrence love and sex are almost identical, one seems
impossible without the other, but although love, for him, can be just
another name for sex, there is also a non-sexual aspect to some of the
relationships in *Sons and Lovers*. Miriam feels that she is the caretaker
of Paul's soul and to some extent she is right; algebra lessons, we have
seen, can be given sexual overtones, but not all of the studying and talking that Paul and Miriam do is undermined like this. Then, of course,
there are the male relationships he forms, notably with Edgar Leivers,
which, although sensual, are not sexual. Later, in *Women in Love* and
elsewhere, Lawrence developed his idea of masculine relationships to
a point where a sexual content enters in, but this is not apparent in *Sons
and Lovers*.

Sons and Lovers is an adolescent novel in that it deals with the problems of a young man. As a result, although the possibility of marriage
does appear briefly on Paul's horizon, the central issues are sex and love
and his development can be charted in terms of women, starting with
his mother.

Religion, Christian and otherwise

Lawrence, like Paul Morel, was brought up as a Protestant Christian
and in fact attended a Congregationalist chapel as a young man. He
gradually moved away from Christianity, however, and in *Sons and
Lovers* we can see how he developed his own religious view of the world
in a way rather different from that of his early days.

In this novel Miriam represents Christianity. She and Paul are often at chapel together and, as we have seen, she is 'intense' and 'soulful'. She is often described in angelic terms and Lawrence says that 'there seemed an eternal maidhood about her' which associates her with Mary, the virgin mother of Christ. This sort of religion is, of course, rejected by Paul. He becomes unable to bear Miriam's concern for his soul and his relationship with her fails because she has too much soul and not enough body.

Interestingly, Miriam, who is soul and Christianity, is offered as a 'sacrifice' to Paul's sensuality. She almost feels it to be a religious duty to give herself to him and in this passage from Chapter 11 we can see the movement between one religion and the other, between Christianity and Lawrence's own religion:

> There was something divine in it; then she would submit, religiously, to the sacrifice, He should have her. And at the thought her whole body clenches itself involuntarily, hard, as if against something; but Life forced her through this gate of suffering, too, and she would submit.

Here Lawrence's vocabulary is interesting: 'divine', 'religiously', 'sacrifice', 'suffering' all remind the reader of the sacrifice of Christ. But Lawrence felt that Christianity was a negative, cold, weak, deathly religion that put death (Christ's sacrifice) above life, so he sets against Miriam's negative coldness the word 'Life', with a capital letter, to proclaim his own religion.

In general Lawrence's religion, although it is often confused and confusing, affirms Life, passion, energy, sex, and impersonal communion with Nature against death and negativity. Man 'unconscious', man in communion with nature, man as an animal, are set above man as 'soul'. In *Sons and Lovers* there are frequent passages of natural description, of flowers for instance, that try to capture the mystery and the beauty of life. Most beautiful and mysterious of all is human flesh: if the strongest impression the novel leaves on us is of the power and wonder of sexual fulfilment it is not because Lawrence was obsessed by this in itself, but because in final intention the novel is a manifesto for Life against death, and Life is at its most 'concentrated', to use his word, in the moment of passion.

Part 4

Hints for study

Points to select for detailed study

1. The brilliant, realistic presentation of the Morel household in the first four chapters of the novel, including Lawrence's frequent use of dialogue and his ability to mix up different periods of time without confusing the reader. See particularly:

The opening of Chapter 2. (Morel's working life, the details of a miner's day.)

The dialogue in Chapter 3 between Mrs Morel, William and, later, Morel, about William's struggle with Alfred Anthony over the 'cobbler'.

The description in Chapter 4 of young Paul in bed (with Arthur and Annie) listening to the terrifying noises of the wind in the tree outside their new house. Childhood fears depicted very accurately.

(This point is not confined to the first four chapters: see, for example, the passage in Chapter 8 where Mrs Morel washes Morel's back).

2. The many passages, in the later chapters, where Lawrence tries to find a style and a vocabulary suitable to the description of love-making. See particularly:

Miriam giving herself in Chapter 11 (notice the cherry-picking episode, with its symbolism).

Clara and Paul first making love in Chapter 12 and their later passion in Chapter 13.

3. Besides these two main points there is a number of significant smaller episodes. Notice the variations in Lawrence's style in these examples:

(1) Paul is interviewed at Jordan's. Chapter 5.

(2) Paul on the swing. Chapter 7.

(3) Paul and Miriam in the wood. Chapter 7.

(4) The Morels' reactions to Arthur's becoming a soldier. Chapter 8.

(5) Paul and Clara at the theatre. Chapter 12.

(6) Paul's argument with Baxter Dawes, early in Chapter 13, and, later, their fight.

(7) Mrs Morel's death—Paul's reaction. End of Chapter 14.

(8) The last pages of the novel. 'Derelict'.

Useful quotations

(*The numbers refer to the chapter in which the quotations can be found*)

Paul:

'Usually he looked as if he saw things, was full of life, and warm.' (5).

'He had shovelled away all the beliefs that would hamper him, had cleared the ground, and come more or less to the bedrock of belief that one should feel inside oneself for right or wrong.' (5).

'He was like so many young men of his own age. Sex had become so complicated in him that he would have denied that he ever could want Clara or Miriam or any woman whom he . . .'. (10).

[Paul speaking of women:] 'They seem to want *me*, and I can't ever give it them.' (13).

Miriam:

'She had a beautiful warm colouring . . . (6).

'She wanted to prove that she was a grand person like the . . . 'Lady of the Lake' . . . (6).

'The girl was romantic in her soul.' (7).

'Miriam seemed as in some dreamy tale, a maiden in bondage, her spirit dreaming in a land far away and magical.' (7)

'All the life of Miriam's body was in her eyes . . . (etc).' (7).

'She did not fit in with the others; she could very rarely get into human relations with anyone.' (7).

[Paul says to her:] 'You aren't positive, you're negative.' (9).

[Mrs Radford says of her:] 'She'll never be satisfied till she's got wings and can fly over everybody's head.' (10).

'There seemed an eternal maidenhood about her.' (11).

[Clara says of her:] 'What I hate is the bloodhound quality in Miriam.' (12).

Paul and Miriam:

'He was a long time before he realised her.' (7).

[Paul's sexuality is a threat to Miriam:] 'There was a serpent in her Eden.' (7).

'"Why can't you laugh?" he said.' (8).

'All his passion, all his wild blood, went into this intercourse with her, when he talked and conceived his work. She brought forth to him his imaginations.' (8).

'Miriam was the threshing-floor on which he threshed out all his beliefs.' (9).

'She took all and gave nothing, he said.' (11).

[Paul says to Miriam:] 'You love me so much, you want to put me in your pocket. And I should die there smothered.' (15).

Paul and Miriam and Mrs Morel:

'And he felt dreary and hopeless between the two.' (8).

Mrs Morel and Paul:

'Mrs Morel's intimacy with her second son was more subtle and fine, perhaps not so passionate as with her eldest.' (4).

'His life-story, like an Arabian Nights, was told night after night to his mother. It was almost as if it were her own life.' (5).

[Paul cleans his mother's boots:] 'With as much reverence as if they had been flowers.' (6).

'The mother and son were in ecstasy together.' (6).

'There was one place in the world that stood solid and did not melt into unreality: the place where his mother was.' (9).

[When Paul puts on some of the dead William's clothes:] 'He was alive and hers. The other was dead.' (10).

'He had a life apart from her—his sexual life. The rest she still kept.' (13).

'He kissed her again . . . as if she were a lover.' (13).

'Paul felt crumpled up and lonely. His mother had really supported his life . . . Now she was gone.' (14).

'"Mother!" he whispered—"mother!"' (15).

Mrs Morel and William:

'He was accustomed to having all his thoughts sifted through his mother's mind.' (6).

Mrs Morel and Morel:

'She despised him, and was tied to him.' (1).

'His nature was purely sensuous, and she strove to make him moral, religious.' (1).

'There was this deadlock of passion between them, and she was stronger.' (2).

'Morel watched her shyly. He saw again the passion she had had for him. It blazed upon her for a moment.' (8).

Morel:

'He danced well, as if it were natural and joyous in him to dance.' (1).

'He was like the scotch in the smooth, happy machinery of the home.' (4).

'He was an outsider. He had denied the God in him.' (4).

'Everything deep in him he denied.' (14).

Clara and Paul:

[When they make love, for Paul:] 'There was no himself.' (12).

'She's lost like a grain of sand in the beach . . . Why does she absorb me?' (13).

[After they have become lovers:] 'Her passion for the young man had filled her soul . . . It was almost as if she had gained *herself*.' (13).

The effects of Nature:

'The beauty of the night made him want to shout.' (11).

Sex:

'The highest of all was to melt out into the darkness and sway there, identified with the great Being.' (11).

'To be rid of our individuality . . . that is very beautiful.' (11).

'They were both very still, having known the immensity of passion.' (13).

'It was as if they had been blind agents of a great force.' (13).

'He became, not a man with a mind, but a great instinct.' (13).

Lawrence's religion?:

'Damn your happiness! So long as life's full, it doesn't matter whether it's happy or not.' (10).

How to arrange material to answer questions on 'Sons and Lovers'

As the quotations listed above show, Lawrence is highly 'quotable'. There are dozens of other sentences and passages in the novel which can be quoted to good effect. So the first thing to do when making points about *Sons and Lovers* is to let Lawrence speak for you if possible.

Lawrence does not move according to a cold logic; he is a passionate and immediate writer. As a result his ideas develop during the novel so that in places he seems to be contradicting himself; for example Miriam represents the deathly negativity of Christianity (in Lawrence's view) but in the first quotation given concerning her she is described as 'warm', which seems to contradict her symbolic value. In fact the tragedy is that although she *is* beautiful and 'warm' it is precisely this that her soulful Christianity is denying. So you should try to allow for *both sides* of any aspect of Lawrence. It is usually clear which side he is on, but he does not always stick to it rigidly.

More than with most novels, you should discuss *Sons and Lovers* in terms of *character*. The novel is deeply and primarily concerned with Paul's soul and the interaction between Paul and the other characters. Think hard about what each character *represents* and about what they do to or for Paul.

On the other hand no novel is simply a psychology text-book. *Sons and Lovers* is written in a definite style and in answering almost any question on the novel you should consider Lawrence's *way* of writing, his vocabulary, his repetitiveness, the varying tones of his prose.

Specimen questions

1. Themes

(1) This is a novel about the battle between flesh and spirit. Discuss.

(Answer to include: Symbolic status of Clara, as flesh, and Miriam, as spirit; neither flesh by itself nor spirit by itself is enough for Paul although he is *happier* with Clara than with Miriam; does Lawrence in fact really distinguish between flesh and spirit? His idea of love brings the two ideas together.)

(2) Willey Farm seems as if it is going to become important to Paul, but it does not quite fulfil this. What is Lawrence's attitude to the Nature that Willey Farm represents?

(See Chapter 7; think of the constant references to flowers in the novel; consider Lawrence's treatment of Clifton Gorge (Chapter 12), the view from Nottingham Castle (Chapter 10), and, of course, the many episodes at Willey Farm itself).

(3) Lawrence offers what seems to be a coherent view of the world; in fact it is a confused mixture of different elements.

(Throughout the novel Lawrence, or Paul, seems to be preaching at us; what is he saying? How does he think man should live? Does the novel in fact come to a conclusion? See the last pages.)

2. Character

(1) Lawrence sympathises so much with Paul that he only presents us with a biased view of Miriam/Clara/Mrs Morel/Morel.

(Consider whether Lawrence ever presents the other characters independently, or whether they are always seen through Paul's eyes; obviously Mr and Mrs Morel *are* independent at least in the early chapters of the novel; but Miriam and Clara are perhaps only reflections of Paul.)

(2) Mrs Morel is portrayed with great care, but does the reader, in the end, sympathise with her /like her/ admire her?
(See especially the chapter relating her death, Chapter 14).

(3) Miriam is more than the romantic dreamer that Lawrence suggests. Is there any evidence for this statement?
(See especially Chapters 7 and 11).

3. Structure
(1) Account for the division of the novel into two unequal parts.
(What is Paul's position in the two parts?)

(2) Everything in the novel relates directly to Paul. Without him the book is nothing.
(Consider (*a*) the independence or otherwise of Miriam, Clara, Mrs Morel, and (*b*) the status of such minor characters as Annie, Arthur, William, Leonard.)

(3) The novel repeats the same patterns several times.
(Paul and his mother parallel William and Mrs Morel and, perhaps, Morel and Mrs Morel; Dawes is like Morel in his relationship with his wife; etc.)

4. Language
(1) What is the purpose behind Lawrence's use of dialect?

(2) Lawrence's language varies through the novel. Identify his different styles and account for them.

5. Imagery
(1) Discuss Lawrence's use of Christian imagery in the novel.
(Look out for all the references to 'communion', 'ascension', etc., and to Christian paintings/objects/themes.)

Part 5

Suggestions for further reading

The text

Sons and Lovers is published by Heinemann, London, and in paperback by Penguin Books, Harmondsworth, 1948.

Other works by D.H. Lawrence

Phoenix, Heinemann, London, 1936 and *Sex, Literature and Censorship*, Heinemann, London, 1955. In these essays Lawrence expanded many of the ideas that are evident in his novels.

MOORE, HARRY T. (ED.): *The Collected Letters of D.H. Lawrence*, Two volumes, Heinemann, London, 1962. In his letters Lawrence speaks at his most personal and passionate level.

Biography

MOORE, HARRY T.: *The Priest of Love*, Heinemann, London, 1974. A substantial and detailed account of Lawrence's life which throws a lot of light on the social and personal background to his novels.

Criticism

BEAL, ANTHONY: *D.H. Lawrence*, (Writers and Critics series) Oliver and Boyd, Edinburgh and London, 1961. A good starting point. A brief and clear study of the main aspects of Lawrence's work.

HOUGH, GRAHAM: *The Dark Sun*, Gerald Duckworth, London, 1956. A paperback edition is published by Penguin Books, Harmondsworth. This is a close, detailed study of the features of Lawrence's style. Strong on critical analysis of passages.

LEAVIS, F.R.: *D.H. Lawrence, novelist*, Chatto and Windus, London, 1955. A paperback edition is published by Penguin Books, Harmondsworth. This pioneering study has the merit of taking Lawrence as seriously as he deserves, both as a writer and a social reformer.

MOORE, HARRY T.: *D.H. Lawrence: the Man and his Works*, Forum House, London, 1969. Includes biographical material and gives some insight into all the major works. Especially good on *Sons and Lovers*.

The author of these notes

LANCE ST JOHN BUTLER was educated at Pembroke College, Cambridge. He taught English in Iraq, Algeria and London before working for a year as a banker in Brazil. He was a lecturer in English at King Abdulaziz University, Jeddah, Saudi Arabia (1970–71), then a post-graduate student at the University of East Anglia (1971–72) before becoming a lecturer at the University of Stirling in 1972. He has edited *Thomas Hardy after Fifty Years* (1977) and written *Thomas Hardy* (1978).